An Unplanned Christmas

LIZZIE SHANE

This is a work of fiction. Names, characters, places, brands, media and incidents are either the product of the author's imagination or are used fictitiously. Any resemblance to actual events or persons, living or dead, is entirely coincidental.

ISBN: 9781075917776

CHAPTER ONE

September

Rachel Persopoulos didn't believe in love at first sight. In fact, she was skeptical on the entire concept of love—especially love conquering all. In her experience, love was much more likely to be an excuse for patently idiotic behavior than it was to be the cause for any triumphant happily-ever-after. Men lied, women believed them, idiocy ensued. Lather, rinse, repeat.

Which was why there was absolutely no logical explanation for the fact that Rachel Leigh Persopoulos, Founder and President of the Colorado Chapter of Romantic Cynics R Us, was completely, stupidly, head-over-heels in love.

It was all Cam's fault.

He wasn't the man of her dreams. There were no men in her dreams. Her dreams were much too practical for that. She was a planner, and she had a five-year plan to become Colorado's premiere event coordinator—starting with her interview tomorrow for TD Events and culminating when she opened her own event planning business. Maybe someday she'd even take it national, but she wouldn't need a man to do it.

All her life she'd seen her mother rely on men, believe in men, and be disappointed by men. She wasn't going to be her mother.

Luckily, Cam was nothing like her father. Well, they were both professional athletes—which had given her pause at first—but three-and-a-half weeks into the best September of her life, she knew now that was where any similarity ended.

He was funny. He was charming—and okay, yes, her father had been those things too, but Cam was also *honest*. Blunt and unashamed. He simply said whatever he was thinking and took the consequences. So confident in who he was, so comfortable making mistakes, letting them roll right off him—which for a perfectionist like Rachel was a novel concept.

They were so different—but he was everything she hadn't realized she'd always needed.

She'd always thought her mother was unbearably naïve for trusting her father, but here she was, falling for someone. Trusting him. Loving him.

Love.

It was such a weird word. She loved her mother. She loved her grandmother. But she'd never said it to a man before. Never even *thought* it about a man before.

He'd said it this morning. The L word.

"You don't have to say it back," he'd murmured, tucking a lock of hair behind her ear. "I just knew if I didn't tell you I'd spend all day wishing I had and if I'm distracted thinking about you, how am I going to focus on destroying the Diamondbacks?"

His grin had been so easy, that cocky confident smile that had wormed its way into her heart.

"I guess I might be somewhat fond of you," she'd teased—and he'd laughed, his mouth still curved when he started kissing her senseless.

And it did feel like she'd lost all her sense. Such a cliché. The girl who didn't believe in love falling harder than anyone.

She glanced down at the numbers on her ticket. She'd never been interested in sports, but she'd recently started learning her way around ballpark seating charts. Being whisked off to San Francisco for a weekend series wasn't a bad baseball initiation, but this was her first home game and it felt more real somehow. Less like a fairy tale getaway and more like it could actually be real life.

The causeways were crowded even though the game wouldn't start for another twenty minutes. Cam had said it wasn't always like this, but playoff fever had gripped the city and now every game was humming with excitement. They were "in the hunt"—a fact local sports reporters kept attributing to Cam's electric September, though he changed the channel any time anyone mentioned his streak, muttering direly about jinxes when anyone dared speak the words "free agency."

Still, Rachel had heard enough to know that he was on the brink of something big. Something that might mean a major pay raise and a move to LA.

She knew he was worried it would all go up in smoke—baseball players took superstition to new levels—so they hadn't talked about LA. But she'd started to think about California. She'd told herself she would never be the kind of woman who made major life decisions because of a guy, but there had to be even more opportunities for event planners in LA than there were in Denver and Boulder. *Somebody* had to run all those fancy Hollywood premieres and after parties. Why not her?

Rachel had never been impulsive, but with Cam it didn't feel like a risk. It felt like all the little cogs of her life clicking neatly into place. As soon as she'd let herself fall for him, everything had fallen together. Cam would get the free agent deal he wasn't letting himself hope for, she would be the next big thing in event planning, and maybe in a few years, when her career was on steady footing, they could think about starting the big family part of her had always secretly wanted.

He called her his good luck charm, attributing all his September success to her, but she knew he worked harder than anyone else. He deserved this. And so did she, dang it. Hadn't she earned a little perfect in her life?

The crowd swelled around her and Rachel stepped out of the way of what looked to be an entire Little League team—nearly bumping into a table that had been set up at the edge of the concourse.

"Whoops! Watch out, honey."

A tall, slim woman caught her arm, steadying her when she would have stumbled into a massive display of baseball souvenirs. "Sorry." She glanced at the woman, smiling ruefully. "I'm not used to these crowds."

"No harm done. Buy a raffle ticket and all is forgiven." She flashed a smile to show she was joking. Stunningly gorgeous from her perfectly made up face to the thick curls tumbling around her shoulders, she was wearing a team jersey and standing in front of a banner reading *Rockies Wives Charities*.

Rachel flushed, suddenly nervous as she realized this must be the wife of one of Cam's teammates. She hadn't met any of them yet. Everything between her and Cam was so new. They'd been existing in their own little romance bubble for the last three weeks—families, friends, all of that would come later.

Now, apparently.

"I'm Rachel." She extended a hand, feeling underdressed in the oversized jersey Cam had given her to wear with her hair tugged into a sloppy ponytail beneath a purple Rockies cap. The one day she didn't do her hair.

"Marta Cruz. Second base." Marta smiled easily, shaking her hand and then gesturing back to the table. "Care to check out some of our silent auction items? We have signed baseballs, signed jerseys that were worn in actual games, you name it. The auctions close in the seventh inning and all proceeds go to support local charities."

Rachel's gaze caught on another woman behind the table wearing a "Cole" jersey with a giant number five on the back. It wasn't the first one she'd seen. Cam must be one of the most popular players, if the jerseys were anything to go by. But this one was pink—and the gorgeous blonde wearing it was also wearing a diamond ring the size of a small planet on her left hand.

Marta noticed the direction of her gaze and grinned. "That's our fearless leader, Erika Cole. She's responsible for organizing ninety percent of what you see here."

Marta kept talking, but suddenly Rachel couldn't hear her past the ringing in her ears. "Erika *Cole*?"

A sister. It had to be his sister. He'd said he had three. It couldn't be…

"Our catcher's wife." Marta beamed, oblivious to the havoc she was wreaking on Rachel's equilibrium as the bottom fell out of her world. "I see you're wearing a Cam jersey. Big fan? Erika's the sweetest. I'm sure she'd be happy to talk to you. And I think we have a couple of signed Cam items in the silent auction today—"

Marta turned toward the table—

—and Rachel dove back into the crowd, moving fast.

She didn't know where she was going. *Away.* Anywhere but here. She couldn't breathe and pressed a hand to her chest. Her heart was pounding—a heart attack. She might actually be having a heart attack. A panic attack was more likely, but did panic attacks feel like a three ton weight had just been slammed on top of your chest?

He was *married.*

Of course he was.

No wonder she hadn't met his family and friends. No wonder he'd only invited her to the away games before today.

Did his wife know about the condo where Rachel had woken up with him this morning? Where did she think he'd spent last night? Rachel spun to march back to the fundraiser table in a fit of sisterhood to tell his wife the truth—but she'd gotten turned around in the crowd and couldn't figure out where she'd been.

And then the tears were blurring her vision so much that she couldn't see anything at all. Swarms of people surged around her as the PA system boomed over the ringing in her ears, announcing the line-up, *"Batting fourth, the catcher, CAMERON COLE!"*

The crowd responded with a roar and Rachel reeled, slapping a hand over her mouth as her stomach revolted. She stumbled into a bathroom, blindly finding her way to a stall and locking herself inside, struggling to keep her sobs silent and her breakfast in her stomach. *I will not make a scene. I will not make a scene.* She wasn't her mother, damn it. She was the calm one. The rational one. She whispered the words over and over in her head like a mantra—but they didn't stop the other words that wanted to drown them out.

He'd made her a mistress.

Just like her mother. She'd sworn she wouldn't be that brand of stupid. She'd *told* Cam about her past, about her father and his lies. He'd been sympathetic, the asshole. He'd worked so freaking hard to earn her trust—and she'd been so certain that he wouldn't put in all that work if he wasn't on the level. That no baseball player who could crook his finger and have a new girl every night of the week would bother with someone who made him work as hard as Rachel had. Not if he wasn't the real deal. Not if he had a wife at home.

She shouldn't have trusted him. Emotion caught in her throat and she stifled a sob.

She fished out her phone. He wouldn't have his on him. He left it in the locker room during games. He wouldn't know for hours that he'd been found out.

Unless this was what he'd wanted when he invited her to this game. He had to know his wife would be there.

His *wife*.

She'd thought they were building something together. She'd started dreaming about a future with him. God, she'd been so *stupid*.

She typed the words—the only two words she would give the asshole before she blocked his number and evicted him from her thoughts. The only two words that were echoing through her head. Her throat burning and moisture streaking tracks down her cheeks, she hit send.

It's over.

CHAPTER TWO

Two years later, December

Rachel hated surprises.

In her experience, even when they looked good at first glance, they almost always came with a catch. She much preferred her life to be carefully planned, neatly organized, and surprise free. So when her boss texted her as she was walking into the building with *Come straight to my office when you get in,* her stomach immediately pitched down toward her toes.

One of the best things about working for Trista Dale Events was that Trista didn't like surprises any more than Rachel did. Everything in the office was beautifully, efficiently planned well in advance. The other best thing was that her hours were flexible—so when her life erupted into chaos, as it had developed an unfortunate habit of doing lately—she could work from home or make up the hours later. Which was why it was nearly noon and she was only now walking into the historic three-story building in downtown Boulder that housed TD Events.

The lobby was decked out in full Christmas cheer—which should have put her in the spirit of the season, but all it did this morning was remind her that all of her own Christmas decorations were still neatly packed in her storage locker, waiting for her to get around to putting them up. It was only the first week of December, but Rachel had always put up her tree and decorated her place on the day after Thanksgiving. The fact that she hadn't gotten around to it over a week later was hanging over her, making her feel like she was running behind on everything in her life.

This was the first Christmas Sofie might actually have some inkling what was going on. Rachel had wanted this year to be perfect, to set the precedent for all the Christmases to come, but life kept getting in the way. She felt like she'd been running late for two years—just a few steps behind where she wanted to be at all times. Like feeling caught up and in control of her life was a luxury she could no longer afford.

Taking the stairs, since the time to go to the gym was another bygone luxury, she jogged up the two flights to the TD Events offices. Most of their clients didn't come here, preferring to have the Trista Dale Team come to them, but the office was still a showplace. Classy. Refined. Flawlessly organized.

It always made Rachel feel calmer—her oasis of a neatly ordered world.

Her throat tightened at the thought of the text, but she forced down the flash of nerves. She was good at her job. Trista liked her. She was *not* being called into the boss's office to be fired three weeks before Christmas. Even if she had been taking advantage of the company's loose schedule more than usual lately.

Sofie had seemed to catch every bug she came into contact with this fall. On the plus side, Rachel had told herself the baby was building a strong immune system—but when Sofie was sick, she got Rachel's mother and grandmother sick, which meant they couldn't watch the baby as they normally did while she was working. And then, of course Rachel had caught the plague herself—

But her events had been perfection. She'd made sure of it. None of the chaos in her home life had affected her work. Her work was the *one* place where things went right. She couldn't lose this job.

She moved quickly to her office, shrugging off her coat and setting her laptop bag on the desk, before smoothing her hair. She never used to wear it up. She'd always been a little vain about her hair, the thick, dark chocolate waves falling over her shoulders, making her feel feminine and flirty. But after cleaning enough spit-up out of her hair to last a lifetime, chignons had become Rachel's hairstyle of choice.

She knew she looked sleekly professional in her pencil skirt and silk blouse—after a hurried wardrobe change this morning when Sofie had somehow managed to smear banana on her dress. Her heels sank into the plush carpet as she made her way toward Trista's office, giving herself a pep talk along the way.

She was probably being assigned a new event. Maybe even a big one. More responsibility. A raise. The text could be any number of good things. Trista had loved the ideas she'd come up with for the Russell House fundraiser at last week's staff meeting. This was probably about that. A pat on the back. A bottle of champagne.

Though Rachel had sworn off champagne after a certain event two years ago. She hadn't even had that much to drink, just a couple glasses, but her judgement had clearly been compromised because Rachel Persopoulos was *never* impulsive, *never* threw caution to the wind, and *never* fell head over heels for a guy she barely knew. Her mother had lobbied that Sofie should have been named Cristal—after the reason she was conceived—but Rachel had never confessed that it was the guy, more than the two glasses of champagne, that had made her feel so fizzy and deliciously reckless that night. Hell, that entire three and a half weeks. She'd been intoxicated by Cam.

More the fool her. He hadn't turned out to be who she thought he was at all.

Rachel smothered the thought, evicting *him* from her brain. She didn't think about him. He didn't matter. He wasn't in the picture. Period.

Her boss's admin assistant wasn't at her desk, but Trista's office door was open, her voice drifting out. Probably on the phone. Her own phone in hand, ready to make notes on whatever project Trista was probably assigning her, Rachel tapped on the doorframe as she popped her head inside to let her boss know she was here.

Except Trista wasn't on the phone. A client sat opposite her desk. A large, broad-shouldered, dark-haired man in a sport coat.

"Ah. Here she is," Trista said, breaking off what she was saying with a smile. Her boss rose as the man turned—

And all the oxygen whooshed out of the room.

Not just a client.

Cameron Cole.

All-Star catcher. Local hero. Beloved by one and all. Handsome, rich, talented.

And Sofie's father.

Sofie's *very married* father.

She was hallucinating. That had to be it. But Trista was rounding her desk, smiling as if Rachel wasn't having a coronary on the spot, and Cam was rising from his chair, recognition flashing over his face before he erased the expression.

"Rachel, I'd like you to meet Cameron Cole—"

"We've met," Rachel blurted—then immediately regretted the words. She did *not* want to explain to her boss how she knew Cam. "So good to see you again," she said with what she hoped was professional poise, thrusting her hand at him in an attempt to prevent Trista from asking where they'd met. "I thought you'd moved to LA."

It had been part of the reason she hadn't. Her half-brother lived there and last year she'd been offered a job with an incredibly prestigious wedding planner who was looking to expand their business—but she hadn't wanted to risk running into Cam. She knew LA was a huge city, but she'd had a recurring nightmare about bumping into him while walking with Sofie in the park. It had kept her up nights until she turned down the job offer and decided to stay in Boulder.

"I did," he confirmed—his voice the same deep, distinctive tone that still haunted her dreams. There was something about his voice—it always sounded layered to her, with an extra rasp that cranked the sex appeal up to eleven and made the little hairs rise on her arms. As they were doing now. "But I'm back for the off-season. Colorado will always be home and I'm still connected to the community here."

His pale grey eyes searched hers and she tried not to let her panic show in her gaze. What was he trying to say? *Connected* to the community? Could he mean a genetic connection? Did he know about Sofie?

Not that she was trying to hide her from him, but she didn't want her daughter to grow up feeling about her cheating ass of a deadbeat father the way Rachel had always felt about hers. Better to keep him out of her life entirely.

"Cameron is one of our celebrity victims for the Bachelor Auction at the Russell House fundraiser."

Rachel jerked, dropping Cam's hand abruptly as she became aware of her boss's presence again. "Bachelor?" she blurted, unable to keep the skepticism out of her voice, but Trista didn't seem to register it.

Trista turned, her body language steering them all back to the seating area in front of the desk. "He's also agreed to be the face of our last promo push to raise awareness for the event. There's a photo shoot with all the bachelors this afternoon and we've arranged to have a reporter from a local lifestyle magazine sit down with him after for an interview."

There was that word again. Bachelor. Trista really needed to do more research on her so-called bachelors, or some unsuspecting bidder might get her hopes up only to find out he was married the hard way—by bumping into his wife, like Rachel had, on the same day the lying bastard told her he was in love with her.

Cam resumed his seat and Rachel forced her body to act naturally, sinking down onto the other chair facing the desk. Trista leaned against it. "I figured you were the best person to brief him on the details of the event, since so many of the ideas were yours and you'll be taking over the final preparations while I'm out of town."

Rachel tried to keep the shock off her face since Trista clearly intended to play this off for Cam as something that had been part of the plan all along, but this was the first she was hearing about Trista going anywhere or her taking over anything.

The Russell House fundraiser was huge. Easily one of the biggest events they handled every year. Rachel had done several smaller events on her own and helped with the major ones, but she'd never actually been in charge of one of the tent-pole events before. Her breath went short at the heady surge of pride that Trista would trust her with this.

Though that still didn't explain where her boss was going.

That would have to be a question for another time. Rachel kicked into work mode, her smile smooth as she faced Cam. "Absolutely. I'd be happy to answer any questions you have."

Cam's grey eyes met hers and a little zing of panic shot down to her chest at the look in them. She should have been more specific that she was only answering questions about the event—but Trista stepped in before he could speak.

"Perfect." She beamed, evidently happy that Rachel had played her part well. "Cameron needs to head to the photoshoot now so we can get him started on hair and make-up and I need to have a quick word with you, Rachel, but then you can head along to the shoot." She turned her attention fully on Cam. "Rachel can answer any of your questions there. And you already have her number if you think of any other questions or concerns over the next few days. She'll be your point person during the press push."

Cam had been unusually quiet—she didn't remember him being nearly mute, but then how well had she really known the man? The sum total of their relationship had been three whirlwind weeks—starting with too much champagne at a charity gala and ending with that disastrous ballgame.

He stood now, straightening his cuffs, his eyes never leaving hers. "I look forward to it," he murmured in that raspy sex god voice—and her panic level hit critical as she tried to decipher what he meant by that.

She rose as well, hoping her movements didn't look as jerky and wooden as they felt. She automatically shook his hand when he finished shaking Trista's. It was the second time she'd touched him, but this time her initial shock had retreated enough that she could actually feel her fingers—and his. His hands were large and calloused and warm. Incredibly warm.

She remembered that now. A little detail she'd forgotten in the last two years. His hands had always been hot where hers were cold. He would chafe her hands between his, absently, without even seeming to notice he was doing it, tucking her against him to warm her up.

She jerked back her hand, smiling to cover the abrupt movement. She needed to act naturally. Not just to assure her boss that she was fully capable of taking care of the largest fundraiser on TD Events' Christmas docket, but also to avoid making Cam suspicious. He probably barely remembered her. The last thing she needed was him thinking he was anything more than a random guy she'd hooked up with a few times two years ago.

Casual. She needed to keep it casual.

Trista guided Cam to the door of her office where her admin assistant had reappeared. JoJo beamed and took over the job of showing him out. Trista waited until he was out of earshot and then turned back toward Rachel, closing the door behind her.

"Sorry to spring that on you. Everything all happened at once and I only had the chance to send you the one text." Trista strode back behind her desk, waving Rachel back to the seat she'd vacated.

"What all happened at once?" she asked, trying to ignore the frantic panic rabbit that was bouncing around her brain at Cam's reappearance in her life.

Trista flicked a glance at the photo on her desk. "Apparently I'm going on my honeymoon."

Rachel blinked. "Didn't you get married three years ago?"

"We did," Trista confirmed. "But we never took our honeymoon because we were always waiting for it to be a good time to be away—which isn't entirely my fault. Audrey works as much as I do. But this morning my darling wife issued an ultimatum. Honeymoon or divorce. Apparently she thinks we need drastic measures—which translates to three weeks at some eco-resort in Fiji. Starting next Friday. Which means I need someone else to take over the Russell House Christmas auction. You were the obvious choice—though I would have preferred to talk to you about it before introducing you to the talent. I'm sorry about that. I already had the meeting with Cole scheduled. He was walking in the door as I got off the phone with Audrey confirming the dates."

Her usually unflappable boss sounded more flustered than Rachel had ever heard her—though by most people's standards she was still two Xanax past calm. Rachel leaned forward in her chair, projecting as much confidence as she possessed. "Don't worry about the auction. I've got this."

"I know you do," Trista said. "And I know the timing is terrible—during the holidays when you want to be spending time with your family—but so many of the new features were your ideas, it didn't seem right to offer it to anyone else."

"No, I want to do it," Rachel assured her. If she

proved she could handle a major event like this, more big things were certain to come her way. "I'll have it so organized it will practically run itself. Just concentrate on enjoying your vacation."

Trista smiled. "I knew you were the right person for the job. You already have access to all the files you'll need on the company server. And I'll be here for the next week if you have any questions as you're taking over." Her gaze flicked to the empty chair where Cameron had sat. "How do you know Cameron Cole?"

"Passing acquaintance." Rachel felt her face heating and hoped her blush didn't show. "We met at a charity gala a few years ago—and I'm fairly sure he wasn't eligible for a bachelor auction at the time."

"Ah. He's divorced now."

Shocker. His wife had probably dumped him when she discovered he was a lying, cheating ass.

Rachel ignored the bitter voice in the back of her mind as Trista continued, "Though the Bachelor Auction is less dates and more experiences. I'm still not sure we made the right call by labeling it that."

Rachel vividly remembered that discussion. It had been a coincidence that all the early volunteers donating experiences happened to be single men and the marketing team had latched onto the idea. "I thought *Boulder Life* loved the bachelor angle?"

"They do. But they aren't the ones asking people to shell out a hundred and fifty bucks a plate to attend." She grimaced. "It's your headache now, I guess." She glanced at the clock on her desk. "You should probably head over to the photo shoot. I don't trust Amanda Smith from *Boulder Life* not to arrive early and blindside our boys."

Rachel suppressed her cringe at the reminder that

Cam was expecting her.

She could do this. All she had to do was organize the largest charity event she'd ever coordinated while trying to avoid the lying scumbag sperm-donor—who happened to be the public face of the event.

Easy.

CHAPTER THREE

"Cameron Cole. How is a catch like you still single?"

Because I told a woman I loved her and she broke up with me via text message. Cam smothered the thought, not allowing a trace of it to show on his face. Luckily, he was an expert at catching curve balls and making it look easy. He'd worked with world-class pitchers with ungodly movement who didn't always know where their pitches were going to end up, and he had to be ready for whatever was coming at him because if he didn't get his glove on the ball the ump wasn't going to call it a strike, no matter how nasty it was.

He had a reputation for being unflappable. Superman with nerves of freaking steel. No one saw the effort. He made sure of it.

So he didn't even blink when the little blonde reporter fluttering her lashes at him lobbed that curveball at him. Years of media training kicked in and he smiled enigmatically. "It's a mystery," he said, perpetuating the myth of his charmed life—when what he wanted to do was tell her to check her damn facts.

Because he wasn't *still* single. He was *currently* single because his wife had left him three years ago, immediately after being diagnosed with ovarian cancer. Erika had called it a wake-up call and packed her bags—though the divorce had taken much longer, delayed by her treatment. She'd moved out, but they'd continued to play the part in public—divorced-but-not-really-divorced so she could stay on his insurance.

They really were better as friends. Once his ego had gotten over the blow, he'd had to admit she had a point with the whole *I-think-I-loved-you-because-I-told-myself-I-should* thing, though he'd still been in no position to think about relationships or the future.

So of course he'd fallen ass-over-ears in love.

Fallen so freaking hard and fast it was like something out of a sappy movie. Fast, and hard, and reckless as hell.

Unfortunately it hadn't turned out to be the kind of movie with a happy ending, as he'd discovered when the one woman he'd let himself get close to during the entire messy chemo/separation process had broken up with him via text message with no freaking explanation. Only to pop up two years later, waltzing into the TD Events office this morning and smiling at him as if nothing had happened. As if that crazy September had meant nothing to her.

And maybe it hadn't. Maybe he was the only one who had been hit by the love stick so freaking hard it had been like taking a fastball to the face.

But still, it would have been nice if she'd seemed even a little flustered. Even if that wasn't Rachel. Rachel was composed. Calm. Friggin' gorgeous.

How could he have forgotten how beautiful she was? It wasn't just her features—which were, yes, very symmetric and all that stuff science said was supposed to be objectively attractive. But it was the way she smiled. The way she blushed. The way she looked at him. The way she'd always looked at him. Like she couldn't look away. The two of them caught in the same gravitational pull.

Though maybe that had just been wishful thinking.

She certainly seemed capable of looking away now. Without moving his head, so he didn't upset the work being done by the make-up artist, he glanced over toward where Rachel was speaking to the other bachelors, her back to him and her phone in her hand. She'd been supposed to brief him on the details of the fundraiser before the little blonde piranha arrived, but Blondie had been early and she'd latched onto him before he'd had a chance to do more than sit in the make-up chair for the photo spread.

He'd done a few print ads over the years, so he knew the drill. Let people fuss over him for an hour or so, then clench his jaw for the cameras. Easy.

What wasn't so easy was keeping his mind on the questions the little piranha was asking when he couldn't seem to stop stealing glances at Rachel.

"C'mon, Cam," the reporter cooed. "Our readers want to know. Commitment issues? Or did someone break your heart?"

Cam's gaze flicked over to Rachel again.

He didn't see what any of this had to do with Russell House or their cancer research efforts—wasn't this supposed to be for a lifestyle magazine, not a tabloid? But since Rachel didn't look like she was going to save him anytime soon, he played nice with the little reporter. "I guess I'm still looking for the One," he said with an easy smile.

Always easy. The perfect illusion of his charmed life. *Pay no attention to the man behind the curtain.*

The make-up artist tsked softly and he relaxed his face so she could work on it.

"And you're going to find that One at a bachelor

auction?"

"Hey, you never know when you're going to meet Ms. Right." He'd met Rachel at a cystic fibrosis fundraiser. "Really, I'm just trying to support an organization I believe in—and if I meet some new friends in the process, all the better."

The piranha sighed, reluctantly letting him steer the conversation toward the fundraiser she was supposedly there to write a story about. "Have you been a supporter of—" She glanced down at her notes. "—the Russell House long?"

"For several years now." He stopped himself from saying his ex-wife had been treated there after she left him—somehow he didn't think that was the soundbite they wanted. "The teams I've played for have always been very involved in the local communities and Russell House is an incredible organization."

"Uh-huh." The piranha made an absent note on her pad. "Speaking of your new team, rumor has it you've been seen with a number of Hollywood actresses since your move to Los Angeles. Any comment?"

A new voice spoke behind him. "Let's stick to the fundraiser, shall we?" Rachel suggested lightly as she appeared at his side.

Cam's relief at her intervention was matched only by his irritation over the question she'd heard. As far as he knew there were no rumors outside of Miss Smith's overactive imagination, but he didn't want Rachel thinking he'd been bragging about his LA exploits.

Not that it mattered what she thought. She'd broken things off with a freaking *text*. It would serve her right if he'd been seeing half of the members of the Screen Actors Guild in his spare time—but he was still, stupidly, trying to prove to her that he was one of the good ones. Always trying to prove himself.

"Has Mr. Cole told you about the experience he's auctioning off?" Rachel prompted.

"You're calling it an experience? Not a date?" the reporter asked, her eyebrows arching.

"It's so much more than a date," Rachel said without missing a beat. "Just like the event is so much more than a bachelor auction. Naturally, that's a large part of the evening and it will be a lot of fun for the bidders and spectators alike, but we also have a silent auction and a number of raffles throughout the evening—including the Express Pass. That's a new feature for this year's fundraiser—making the event more exciting for the patrons who want to support Russell House, but may not be able to afford to bid thousands for our bachelors. For the low price of a raffle ticket, attendees can be entered to win the Express Pass, which will be drawn immediately before the live auction begins. The Express Pass winner then gets their choice of any of the Bachelor experiences—so if you'd like to go hiking and paragliding with a famous rock-climber or fly an F-15 with our fighter pilot, you could win the experience of a lifetime for just the cost of a raffle ticket."

"Or you could win a day taking batting practice with me, a private coaching session with dinner afterwards, and two seats in the owner's box on Opening Day, with a signed jersey to wear to the game."

"That does sound like quite a prize," the reporter cooed, fluttering her lashes at him again. "So are there still tickets available?"

"Absolutely." Rachel stepped forward, as if Miss Smith had asked her the question. "I'll give you all the information on how your readers can register for the event, but right now I'm afraid Mr. Cole is needed for the photo shoot. Shall we watch from over here?"

Rachel steered the reporter away from him, smiling calmly and making it sound like she was helping the woman out, giving her the best possible view. She'd always been good at this stuff. It was what had first caught his eye.

The team had bought a table at a cystic fibrosis event and he'd been there with some of the guys—his first event without Erika on his arm. Their marriage had been functionally over for a year by then, but it had still felt odd, being there that night without her. Even when they rarely saw one another during the season, they'd always gone to those kinds of things together, presenting the perfect united front. Even if it was just an illusion. And a habit. His life had been a series of habits and rituals.

And then he'd seen Rachel, calmly ruling the world…

"Mr. Cole? We're ready for you."

Jerked out of his musings, Cam followed the production assistant to the set where he shook hands with the other bachelors. The photographer handed out Santa hats and began arranging them on a series of blocks around a giant Russell House logo and for the next several minutes Cam turned off his brain and followed directions. Sit here, crouch there, smile, don't smile, brood, smirk, fold your arms, flex your arms.

He hesitated when the photographer asked him to take his shirt off—but Rachel proved she'd been paying attention from her perch to one side, stepping forward to speak quietly to the photographer who apparently let himself be convinced they didn't need the rippling pecs photos after all.

Rachel retreated back to the director chairs where she had been sitting with the *Boulder Life* lady—and Cam's gaze followed her.

She looked good in her tight skirt and the silky blouse that made him want to reach out and touch—though the fine fabric would probably snag on his calloused hands. But then she'd looked good in one of his old jerseys and a pair of boxers too. Her hair had been down then—he didn't think he'd ever seen it up before today. Though it looked good like this. Businesslike. She radiated competence—which was sexy as hell.

"Eyes to the left, please, Mr. Cole."

He snapped his gaze back toward the camera, his face heating beneath the make-up.

He needed to keep his head in the game. He was here for Russell House—not to ogle the one who got away. Cam forced himself to focus on what he was doing, putting his all into smoldering for the camera as the photographer finished the group shots and pulled him aside for some close-ups.

The *Boulder Life* piranha swooped in on the other bachelors, her lashes fluttering at Mach two. Rachel apparently didn't think those guys needed babysitting, because she wandered over to a bank of computer screens with one of the photographer's assistants and bent to peer at one of the monitors, her skirt pulling tight across her—

"Mr. Cole? Look right here."

Cam snapped his gaze back to the camera, silently cursing his distraction. What was he doing? She was just a woman. Yes, she was gorgeous—but after eight years in the majors he'd gotten used to women who would normally be out of his league giving him the time of day. Even though he'd been married most of that time and hadn't taken advantage of it. What was so special about

Rachel?

His brain immediately provided flashes of memory to answer the question. Three weeks. That's all they'd had. But each day had been better than the last. They'd talked for hours that first night, so caught up in one another that neither of them had noticed how late it got, or that the hotel staff had cleared the ballroom while they were out on the balcony, enjoying the warm September night.

Everything had been perfect. They'd just *fit.* He'd never clicked with anyone like that, like they'd known one another for decades rather than days.

He'd never been a believer in love at first sight, but he had started to believe with Rachel—

And then she'd been gone. Just like that. She'd come with him on the last road trip of the season and when they got back he'd been thinking forever, but she'd obviously had other plans.

She'd been supposed to meet him after the game that day. They were in the hunt for the playoffs, so close he could taste it. He'd played well, going three-for-four with two RBIs, but they'd still lost—and then he'd gotten the text. Leaving him wondering what the hell had happened.

It would have been one thing if they'd fought. Or even disagreed about *anything*. But things had been pretty damn perfect.

He'd wondered if she'd found out about his ex and jumped to conclusions, but he couldn't stop thinking of how she'd reacted when he'd told her he loved her that morning. When she'd said she was *somewhat fond* of him. Was that why she'd bailed? Because she didn't feel the same?

He'd never known—and maybe that was why he

couldn't stop obsessing about her now. The not knowing. He needed a freaking reason. Closure, right? That was what therapists were always going on about, wasn't it?

She hadn't taken his calls or responded to his texts. She'd always met him or come to his place so he hadn't even known where she lived—which had just reminded him how little he really knew about her. Had she been hiding something? Had something happened to change her mind about him?

His teammates would have told him he was lucky he hadn't wound up married to the rebound chick. That dating while you were getting divorced was a great way to end up with *two* expensive ex-wives on the payroll. But it hadn't felt like a rebound. It had felt like his freaking soulmate. He hadn't even believed in soulmates until then.

He'd finalized his divorce and signed a free agent deal with LA, leaving Colorado behind, but he'd never gotten closure from Rachel. Didn't she owe him that at least?

Now he was back for the off-season, spending time with his family over the holidays and doing the Russell House fundraiser. What better time to hash out unfinished business and move on?

"Perfect," the photographer declared—and he realized he'd been glowering into the camera. Apparently brooding was a good look for these things. "I think we're all set."

Thanking the photographer, Cam handed over the Santa hat and accepted a wipe from the make-up artists, scrubbing gunk off his face—but never taking his eyes off Rachel. She'd avoided meeting his eyes all afternoon, but she couldn't avoid him forever.

They needed to talk.

CHAPTER FOUR

He was watching her.

Rachel tried to focus on the photos flashing across the screen in front of her, but she could feel Cam's gaze tickling the back of her neck and making her want to squirm. She had a job to do and she was going to do it, damn it. Past relationship drama would just have to wait until…never. Never sounded good. She would do her job. He would do his. And they would part ways. End of story.

Except now it was guilt making her squirm. Did she have some obligation to tell him about Sofie? At the time, she'd blocked his number, too wrecked by all the lies she'd stupidly believed to listen to another word from him. When she'd found out she was pregnant, she'd agonized over whether or not to tell him. She'd put it off, telling herself it didn't make sense to reach out to him while she was still in the high-risk first trimester. Then she'd read that he'd taken the job in LA and she'd told herself it was for the best. He was a cheating scumbag. She was doing what was best for her daughter, protecting her from later hurt by not telling him.

But with him here right now, it felt more like a lie.

He was the liar, she reminded herself. He may be divorced now—a fact which apparently hadn't merited the same headlines as his move to LA—but he'd still been very married when he'd been whisking her off on weekend trips to San Francisco to watch him play the Giants. He was *married* when she got pregnant—just like her father had been when her mother conceived her. That apple certainly hadn't fallen far from the tree—no matter how much she might have wished otherwise.

No. He didn't deserve to know. He didn't deserve a damn thing from her. He'd lied to her and used her—

"Rachel?"

She jumped, spinning toward the photographer who was graciously donating his services to Russell House. "Michael. Are we all set?"

"I think we have everything we need." He nodded toward the cluster of bachelors who were gathering up their coats. "They were easy. I'll send along the finals as soon as I've retouched them."

"Thank you. We really appreciate it."

"My pleasure. Anything for a good cause, right?" He went back to gathering up his equipment, and Rachel's attention veered back to the bachelors.

Amanda Smith had latched onto the Air Force pilot, but since he seemed to be enjoying the attention Rachel decided not to intervene. She'd spoken to Amanda during the shoot, providing background on the various bachelors and the experiences they were offering up for the auction. Cam would still be the main bachelor featured in the article, but Rachel had given the reporter carte blanche to include the other men as well. Anything to boost last minute ticket sales. The big bidders and corporate sponsors had already secured their tables, but if they could fill out the ballroom with smaller donors by luring them in with the raffles and the Express Pass, they could make this year's event the most profitable yet. And TD Events would be even more in-demand on the charity circuit.

Once the bachelors had filtered out of the building, taking Amanda Smith with them, Rachel gathered up her bag, thanked the volunteer hair and make-up crew, and headed for the door. Cam was nowhere in sight—which was good. Distance was exactly what she needed.

But as she stepped into the parking lot, a distinctive sex-god rasp spoke at her side. "Walk you to your car?"

Rachel kept her expression polite and her walls up. Civil. "That won't be necessary." *Lying bastard.* She started toward her Hyundai.

Cam fell into step beside her. "I insist."

It was tempting to smack him in the face with her computer bag. Even without her laptop inside, it packed a wallop. But she was being professional. Civil, damn it. "Good work today," she commented, her voice perfectly bland. "I think we got some great shots for the website and the flyers."

"Are we going to talk about this?"

It was trying to snow and a few light, puffy flakes swirled around them. The parking lot was emptying as the other bachelors climbed into their cars and peeled out, but that didn't mean no one could hear them. "About what?" If only she'd arrived early enough to get a closer parking space.

"Us," Cam said baldly, ignoring all her *I-don't-want-to-talk-about-this* signals.

"There is no us."

"There was. Or was that all in my imagination?"

Rachel pursed her lips, walking a little faster. She was determined to focus on her job and the damn man seemed equally determined to dredge up the past.

"Are you really trying to pretend it never

happened?" he demanded, like a dog with a freaking bone.

She shook her head and walked as fast as she dared on the icy pavement, not looking at him. She wasn't sure what she was denying, but she needed to get away from this conversation.

"Rachel."

"What?" she snapped, spinning back to face him, still ten feet from the bumper of her car. Her heel slipped on the ice and only his hand on her arm kept her from taking a hard fall, but she yanked her arm away.

"What happened?" He dropped his hand, something in him seeming to deflate. "I thought things were going so well and then..."

The softness in his eyes tightened her throat—until she remembered he was a *liar*.

"You were *married*," she snapped.

Something flared in his eyes. "How did you find out about that?"

"Are you serious?" she gasped. "*That*. That right there is the problem. Not *no, I wasn't*, but *how did you find out*?"

"That's not—"

"The real question is why I didn't figure it out sooner. I felt like such an idiot because I hadn't even Googled you. It was on your freaking Wikipedia page!"

"Is that why you ghosted on me?"

"It seemed like the logical thing to do when I saw your *wife*." She shook her head, turning to continue toward her car. "You must have thought I was such a sucker. Did you want me to meet her? Is that why you invited me to that game? You must have known she'd be working the Rockies' Wives booth, selling one of your jerseys for the team charities."

"I didn't know. We'd been separated for months—" He sounded more weary than defensive—but in order to be defensive he probably had to acknowledge he'd done something wrong.

She didn't look back. "I told you about my father. I told you why I didn't date athletes."

"Exactly!" His voice was close behind her. "I knew you'd never trust me if I told you I was still technically married—"

"So it's my fault you lied?" she asked incredulously, spinning back to face him.

"We were separated!" The words echoed against the building. "We'd been separated for months. Nearly a year."

"I suppose that's why she was parading around as your wife at Rockies' Wives events? Because that's exactly what people do in the middle of a divorce, right?"

He ran a hand through his hair, mussing it. "She had cancer."

"That's your excuse?" she shouted, no longer caring who heard them. "You couldn't leave her while she was sick? So you'd just cheat on her instead?"

"What? No. She left me. Long before I met you. We weren't telling anyone about the separation because we needed her to stay on my insurance for her treatment—which I would have told you if you'd given me a chance to explain—"

"You had three weeks to explain." She shook her head, shaking away his excuses—her father had always had a ready excuse too. "You should have told me. You knew about my parents. You *knew* I didn't want to be any man's mistress—"

"Which is why I couldn't tell you! It was all so new

and I didn't want to lose you."

"Well, you lost me." She turned toward her car, fishing out her key fob and unlocking it.

"Rachel, *wait*."

She shook her head, unwilling to hear another word. "I just want to get through the next three weeks. This fundraiser is important to me and I will do everything in my power to make it a success and make your experience with TD Events as pleasant as possible, but that's all this is. That's all it can be. Leave the past in the past, Cam."

It wasn't until she was inside her car with the engine running, when she turned to back out of the space and saw the car seat sitting in her backseat that she remembered the *other* little complication in her relationship with Cam.

She hadn't told him about Sofie.

For a moment, in the middle of the fight, she'd actually forgotten about her daughter's relationship to Cam. Actually forgotten who he was.

He'd lied to her, she reminded herself. She gripped the steering wheel and pulled out of the lot, refusing to look to see if he was still standing there watching her go. He may not have meant to hurt her, he may have had his reasons, but he'd lied.

Her father had been like that. A sports legend, but also a genuinely nice guy. Big Aaron, with his big laugh and his big heart. Someone who never wanted to hurt anyone, but still cheated on his wife. A man who would play with his illegitimate daughter and make her laugh until she could barely breathe when he came to visit—but would always fly home to his real family. A man who had supported them when he was alive, but had left them without a freaking dime when he died, so they'd lost the house and had to move back in with her grandmother.

No. Her daughter didn't need a man like that in her life.

Rachel had a plan for Sofie's life. And it didn't include Cameron Cole.

CHAPTER FIVE

Cam had come back to Colorado to spend more time with his family during the off-season, but at the moment the last thing he wanted to do was go to his sister's house for family dinner. The fight with Rachel had him all twisted around.

Her anger had caught him off guard. She *hated* him.

All this time, he'd thought he'd been the injured party. She'd been the one who dumped him without a backward glance—via text, no less. Two hours ago he would have bet his lucky glove she wouldn't even recognize him if she saw him on the street. He never would have predicted she was holding a grudge.

And there was definitely a grudge. Not that he could entirely blame her. He should have told her about Erika. He'd been waiting for the right time—which, in retrospect, was about the dumbest thing he'd ever done in his life.

Cam climbed out of his Range Rover, trying to put the disturbing conversation with Rachel out of his mind as he headed up his sister's driveway. There were already half a dozen other cars crammed into the space—which meant he was likely to take shit for being the last one there, but at least he'd be able to slip out early without having to ask anyone to move a vehicle.

Not that he was already planning his escape—he

loved spending time with his family. It was just that lately being surrounded by his siblings and their perfect nuclear families had started to feel more and more like a reminder of his failures. Especially when none of them could seem to stop talking about how awesome his life was. How freaking charmed. He'd even fooled them.

Cam didn't bother to knock, letting himself in the front door and shedding his coat and scarf. Voices echoed back from the kitchen and living room, but no one had spotted him yet as he ran a hand through his hair.

His grandparents had always hosted the family gatherings when he was growing up, but after his gramps passed away and Gran moved in with his parents, his oldest sister Carly had taken over hostess duties. She'd claimed it was because she had the biggest house with the best entertaining space—which was true—but they all knew the real reason was her compulsive need to be the boss of everything.

"The prodigal son returns!" she called now, spotting him from the kitchen—and he was suddenly surrounded by family, his sisters taking turns hugging him as if he hadn't seen them all a week ago for Thanksgiving.

"So I'm the prodigal now?" he asked as he squeezed Carly. She was nearly a foot shorter than he was, with a smile that lit up her entire face and could turn from sweet to wicked in the blink of an eye.

"You prefer Golden Boy Who Can Do No Wrong? Or Favorite Child, perhaps?"

He rolled his eyes, jerking his chin to where his mother hadn't even looked up from doting on her latest grandbaby to note his arrival. "I think my failure to provide grandchildren officially disqualifies me from favorite child status."

"Point taken." Carly snagged his arm, tugging him to one side. "*Speaking* of popping out grandbabies—"

His eyebrows flew up. "Are you pregnant again?"

"God no. After the twins Eddie got the big V. We are taking no chances."

Cam cringed in sympathy with his brother-in-law. If not Carly… "So Shelby's pregnant? Or Ashley?"

"No. God. No one's pregnant. This is about you. And your future happiness. There's this girl—"

Cam groaned, holding up a hand like a stop sign. "No. Thank you, but no. I do not need to be set up." He started to move away, but Carly latched onto his arm like a bear trap.

"She's a school librarian. Great with kids—"

He tried to shake her off, but she was a tenacious little barnacle. "I can find my own dates. Women do actually like me, you know."

"Yes, but are they the right kind of women?"

Rachel was. Cam kicked that thought to the curb. He did not need to be thinking about the one that got away right now. Even if she was back in the picture for the next few weeks.

"I'm sure you can meet lots of women who make Little Cam stand up and salute—" Carly plowed on.

He cringed. "Please do me a favor and never mention 'Little Cam' to me ever again."

"—but marrying another woman just because she's hot sounds like an excellent way to end up with another ex-wife. We all loved Erika, but none of us were surprised when she left."

"Thank you for that vote of confidence."

"Don't pretend you're offended. You know what I mean. You weren't surprised either."

He couldn't argue with that. Her cancer had shocked him, the divorce not so much.

Carly plowed on. "You need someone who wants the same things you do out of life. Who values the same things you do. Who is sweet and kind and *also* happens to be sexy as hell."

"Which I suppose describes your librarian."

"Of course it does, but that isn't the point. You don't have to date my librarian, but you do need to be getting out there—"

"I get out there plenty." *Bold-faced lie.*

"*And* thinking about how you're picking the women you date. Common interests. Shared goals. What's her five-year-plan?"

"Wow, romantic." When she glared at him, he laughed. "C'mon, Carly. You make it sound like a job interview."

"You never had these conversations with Erika. That's how you wound up married to someone who never wanted kids and assumed you didn't either."

Cam didn't argue that they'd had the conversations—but at the time they'd both been twenty-two and wanting the same things for the distant future hadn't seemed like such a big deal. He'd always figured Erika would want kids eventually, and she'd always assumed the matter was settled. But even if his big sister had a point about their less-than-stellar communication as a couple, there was no way he was going to admit it to her.

He cocked his head as if listening. "Is that one of your children crying?"

"No one's crying. Stop trying to avoid the subject."

"Contrary to what you might think, you aren't actually the boss of my love life."

"But I *should* be," Carly declared without an ounce of doubt and Cam couldn't help but laugh—until his middle sister Shelby appeared at Carly's side.

"Did you tell him about the librarian?"

Cam groaned. "Not you too."

"He doesn't want to be set up," Carly explained before Cam could. "He wants to find his own soul mate."

Shelby snorted as if the idea was ridiculous. "Is that why you're doing this bachelor auction?"

"It's more of an experience auction," he insisted, trotting out the excuse he'd heard Rachel give that afternoon.

"You're doing a bachelor auction, sweetie?" A new voice joined the conversation as his mother appeared, still holding his baby niece, with his youngest sister at her side.

"You're never going to find the right kind of girl if you're auctioning yourself off to the highest bidder like a glorified gigolo," Carly argued.

"It's for charity," he insisted. "And it's just batting practice."

His mother frowned. "Like a test run? To work your way up to real dates?"

"No, the date itself is batting practice," he explained, trying not to read too much into his mother thinking he needed dating practice. "I'm taking the winner to the ball park."

"Romantic," Carly said dryly.

"I think it's a great idea," Ashley spoke up for him, catching her daughter as she lunged from their mother's arms into hers. "Total meet cute material."

"This isn't a rom com," Carly argued. "He needs someone with shared values—"

"I've never understood why you couldn't find the right girl," his mother mused. "You've always had so much going for you."

Cam closed his eyes as the women of his family continued to discuss his dating prospects. Or lack thereof.

It was that interviewer from Boulder Life *all over again. How are you still single, Cam? When are you going to find the One, Cam?*

It wasn't like he wasn't looking.

Admittedly, Erika hadn't been the best choice, in the long run, but he was older and wiser now. He knew what he wanted—or he'd thought he knew. He'd wanted Rachel. He'd been completely gone for her and she'd ghosted on him. It didn't seem to matter how much he supposedly had going for him if the women he got involved with walked away. Like they'd seen through the illusion of his perfect life and didn't want the reality beneath.

Though Rachel hadn't disappeared for any of the reasons his imagination had conjured up. It hadn't been because he'd freaked her out by telling her he loved her and she'd decided she didn't like him after all. She'd left because she thought he was married. Now that she knew the truth…

Could there still be something there? She'd been angry this afternoon, but that had to mean that he still meant something to her, didn't it?

Unless it just meant she hated him.

"I'm not saying he should *marry* whoever wins the bid," Ashley was arguing, louder now. "I just think it's a cute way to meet some single women who obviously have their shit together and support good causes if they have the money to burn at a Russell House fundraiser."

"Money doesn't automatically mean you have your shit together," Carly argued. "Look at Cam."

"Hey."

"Ignore her," Ashley demanded. "She's just bitter because you're going to meet the love of your life at this Bachelor thingy and never want to meet her perfect little school librarian."

"I'm not doing the event to meet women."

"Of course not. You care about cancer stuff," Ashley declared with a disconcerting lack of sincerity. "But if you *also* meet the love of your life—"

"It's going to be the librarian," Shelby insisted. "You haven't met her, Ash. Trust us on this."

Figuring his sisters could easily have this argument without him, Cam sidled away to make his escape, catching his niece automatically as she flung herself into his arms. Gwennie had nothing if not a complete faith that all the adults in her life existed to tote her around and never let her fall—and so far that faith had been upheld.

Cam propped her diaper-padded butt on the crook of his arm and carried her into the living room where the spouses had gathered with the rest of his sisters' offspring. At least here there would be no discussion of his love life.

Or so he thought.

He hadn't been there five minutes before Shelby's husband eyed him over his beer. "So Cam, what's this I hear about you doing a bachelor auction? You really that hard up for a date? I thought that was the whole point of being a professional athlete—so you never had trouble meeting women again."

"Aren't you supposed to be dating some actress in LA?"

"I heard it was a model."

Cam smiled at the good-natured ribbing as his other brothers-in-law joined in. They'd said the right things, all sympathy during the divorce, but they still seemed to believe the rumors that his life was perfect. Which, yes, he encouraged.

He'd cultivated the image of the Golden Boy, like Carly had joked. The guy everything came easily for—so if he didn't have something it must mean he didn't want it, right? Because Cam's life was charmed. He was a natural athlete—or so he'd somehow conned everyone into believing, even his family forgetting that he'd been cut from his high school baseball team. His love life was perfect—and as long as he kept smiling somehow no one noticed that the four-year illusion of his perfect marriage had collapsed when his wife left him. His image was the biggest fraud in baseball—and no one noticed.

They all thought he had everything he'd ever wanted.

But he wanted *this*. The big noisy, nosy family. The baby girl dropping off to sleep on his shoulder. Something to come home to other than an empty house.

And maybe doing a bachelor auction wasn't the best way to meet women—but it had brought him into contact with one woman he couldn't stop thinking about. A woman he was quickly realizing he wasn't nearly as over as he'd thought he was.

He needed to see Rachel again. Maybe just for closure, but maybe…

He hadn't had a chance to adequately explain about Erika and the arrangement they'd had during the divorce. He needed Rachel to understand that he'd meant every word he said to her when they were dating. There might be a chance for them yet. And Cam was not the kind of guy who *ever* gave up until the last pitch in the bottom of the ninth.

CHAPTER SIX

By the time Rachel got home, she was ninety percent sure she had to tell Cam about Sofie. The initial flash of anger had dissipated so she could think again. He was Sofie's father. And, if she believed him, he'd been financially supporting his soon-to-be ex through cancer when they met—which didn't make him the same breed of lying scumbag her father had been.

Though that didn't excuse the lying. Or the fact that he'd actually tried to blame her for the fact that he'd felt like he needed to lie. Or that he'd only seemed concerned with how he got caught and not actually apologetic for the lying and cheating.

Though she wasn't entirely sure it had been cheating. Did it still count if you were only faking staying married? At what moment did it stop being adultery?

Her head hurt just thinking about it as she climbed the steps to the second floor apartment she'd moved into with her mother and grandmother shortly before Sofie was born. She'd needed the support system then, scared of doing the parenting thing on her own, and she'd been reaching for family however she could. She'd even gotten in touch with her father's legitimate son—which had ultimately turned out to be a good thing, though she'd second-guessed sending that letter to Aaron Cross, Jr. a thousand times.

He was the image of their father—not just physically, but as a walking picture of success. A tall, handsome, former-NFL player, just like their dad. But he also appeared to be unfailingly faithful to his fiancée. Which was a big difference from their father. She didn't know of any other half-siblings floating around in the world, but with their father it certainly wasn't impossible that there were a dozen more.

He'd probably told each of their mothers that he loved them. That he was leaving his wife to be with them and only them. That he loved those other illegitimate babies just as much as he loved his legal son. That he hadn't planned any of this, it had just happened, and he couldn't be expected to be held accountable for any of it. It wasn't his fault after all.

Her father. The Great Aaron Cross. Who hadn't even had the courtesy to survive until she was old enough to be mad at him about all the lies—so now she always felt that awful flicker of guilt when she wanted to scream at his memory.

She unlocked the apartment and stepped inside, instantly clapping eyes on the reason she needed to stay far away from men like Aaron Cross and Cameron Cole.

Sofie was strapped into her high chair, shoving pieces of avocado into her mouth—and all over the lower half of her face. Her head turned toward the door and she flung her avocado-covered hands up in greeting, her tiny face lighting up with joy. "Mama!"

"Hi, baby! I missed you!" She made a beeline for her daughter and kissed the top of her head—the only part of her that appeared to be outside the avocado danger zone. "Is that a yummy avocado?"

"Mummy!" Sofie agreed emphatically—and Rachel's heart ached with the strain of containing all the love her sweet girl inspired.

Yaya moved behind Sofie in the tiny galley kitchen, putting the finishing touches on what smelled like moussaka and smiling in greeting. "Hello, *hrisa mou.* Good day?"

"Mm," Rachel mumbled noncommittally. She gave Yaya a one-armed hug before moving to put her laptop bag down in the room she shared with Sofie—and all of Sofie's baby stuff. Thank God for organization or she'd never see the floor.

"I thought this was Mama's shift," she called through the open door as she stepped out of her heels and wriggled her relieved toes in the carpet.

"She had a last minute appointment come up," Yaya explained.

Rachel sincerely hoped the "appointment" was an emergency manicure at the salon where she worked and not a date with whatever deeply unsuitable man she'd fallen for this week.

Since daycare was ludicrously expensive and none of them could afford not to work, Rachel, her mother, and Yaya had worked out a color-coded schedule to show who would watch Sofie at any given time—a strategy she'd stolen from *Jane the Virgin,* since Jane was her organizational soul mate.

And because she practically *was* Jane. If you didn't count the whole virgin thing. They were both living with their mother and grandmother with an unexpected baby. Though thankfully Rachel hadn't had to deal with telenovela levels of drama.

Yet.

There was no telling what would happen now that Cam was back in the picture.

If he was back in the picture.

Could he be back in the picture?

He'd still be in LA during the baseball season, which was more than half the year. She avoided sports, but she'd learned a little about baseball back when she'd actually thought he might be her future. She knew there were two leagues and he now played for the one that meant he wouldn't be playing the Rockies as often during the season.

Would he want them to move to LA so he could see Sofie more? Aaron was there, but it would mean uprooting her mother and grandmother. Could she do that to them? Just for a man who might not even be a good father figure?

Maybe she shouldn't tell him. Keep the status quo. This was good, wasn't it? They were managing just fine on their own. Sofie was happy, and that was all the mattered. Rachel needed to protect that happiness at all costs.

After quickly changing into yoga pants and a faded t-shirt, she emerged from the bedroom and settled into the chair beside Sofie's high chair, making faces at her daughter, who grinned delightedly.

"Your mama didn't know how long she would be." Yaya came out of the kitchen with a plate in each hand, setting one in front of Rachel and settling across the table with the other. Sofie's portion was already sitting on the high chair tray—and being spread across her face.

Rachel knew she shouldn't be relieved that her mother wasn't joining them for dinner, but it was much more peaceful without her. Her mother tended to be a one-woman drama generator and after the day she'd had she didn't have the emotional energy to deal with her.

Rachel's phone binged with a text-alert from her bag

in the other room and she grimaced, setting down her fork. "I should get that. I forgot I owe Aaron a text."

Yaya sighed, her pinched face speaking volumes about her opinions on cell phones at the dinner table, but she didn't say a word until Rachel had grabbed the phone and shot back a quick reply. "And how is your brother?"

It was a strange sentence. A sentence that never would have been spoken in the house two years ago. But it was their strange now. "He's good." Sofie smacked her plastic spoon against her tray and Rachel caught it before she could fling it to the floor. "He and Bree still haven't set a date, and I think they're getting more serious about eloping. I keep thinking I'm going to get a text one day telling me they're in the Caribbean and it's a done deal."

"I'm sure they would tell you beforehand. Is that what the text was about? The wedding?"

Rachel tried not to squirm in her chair. She'd never been able to lie to Yaya—even lies of omission. Her grandmother had a way of looking right through her. "No," she admitted. "He, ah, he invited us out for Christmas."

"Oh." A long pause. "That was nice of him."

The words were carefully bland. Rachel tried not to grimace. It was a nice invitation. Even if all of them knew she could never accept. They were still trying to work out what it was to be family when none of them wanted to put their father's former mistress and his widow in the same room. Not that Aaron's mother wouldn't have been perfectly civil—but no one wanted to rub it in her face and Rachel's mother wasn't exactly known for her tact.

Andromeda Persopoulos, Andie to her friends, was a

strong personality, to say the least. She had a tendency to perform everything she was feeling—or whatever she felt she ought to be feeling—and Rachel invariably found herself embarrassed by the dramatics. She loved her mother, loved her like crazy, but sometimes she could be *exhausting.* Rachel had never understood why everything had to be a show. Why nothing could ever be contained or restrained.

Christmas with her mother was dramatic enough without adding her half-brother and her father's widow to the mix. She wanted a peaceful Christmas this year. A perfectly organized, no drama, no last-minute-disasters Christmas. Her daughter wasn't going to remember every Christmas by what had gone wrong. She probably wouldn't remember this one—Sofie was barely old enough to understand what was going on—but Rachel wanted to set a precedent this year.

Last year they'd spent Christmas at a Chinese restaurant after her mother had tried to make dinner and ended up setting off the fire alarm. She'd insisted on cooking—though Yaya and Rachel had always shared those duties—and accidentally set the self-cleaning oven to clean rather than bake. After the smoke from the turkey filled the kitchen, Andie had joked that at least they got to spend their Christmas with hot firefighters—but it hadn't exactly been the festive holiday Rachel had always dreamed of.

This year would be different.

Especially if Cam was involved.

Rachel's stomach pitched at the thought and she poked at her moussaka rather than taking a bite.

"Are you all right?" Yaya asked, her all-seeing eyes catching the movement.

"I saw Cam today."

Yaya froze, her fork in mid-air, her gaze on her plate. After a moment, she slowly lowered the fork before lifting her eyes to study Rachel's face. "Did you?"

Yaya knew all about Cam. Rachel had told her mother and grandmother about him in gushing terms when they first met—and then in less gushing terms when she'd discovered he had a wife. They knew he was Sofie's father. And they knew that Rachel had never told him—something her mother had always vocally objected to and Yaya had never spoken of one way or the other.

"He's one of the bachelors for the Russell House Auction—which Trista put me in charge of today. We might have to tweak the schedule over the next couple weeks. I may be busier than usual until the auction—"

"Hrisa mou."

Rachel snapped her mouth shut at the endearment, so soft and filled with so much disappointment. She looked away, her eyes landing automatically on Sofie who was chasing a piece of eggplant around her tray with pudgy fingers.

"Bachelor auction?" Yaya asked gently.

Rachel grimaced, still not meeting her eyes. "Apparently he's divorced now."

Yaya made a small sound in her throat.

And of course her mother, with her ever impeccable dramatic timing, chose that moment to sweep through the door.

"Hello, darlings!" Andie called, flinging her scarf onto the hooks by the door with a flourish. Andie never merely entered a room. She made an *entrance*. "The traffic is a nightmare with all this snow. It's a miracle I made it home in one piece." She twirled out of her coat—because God forbid she simply remove the damn thing—and hung it over the scarf. Turning toward them, she became aware of the rigid tension gripping the table and slapped a hand over her heart. "What is it? What's wrong?"

"Cam is back," Yaya said when Rachel couldn't find the words.

"He is?" Andie clasped her hands together, her eyes glowing. "Oh, darling, that's wonderful!"

"No, it isn't," Rachel reminded her—trying to keep the irritation out of her voice for Sofie's sake. The baby had finished her moussaka and was now watching the conversation with wide eyes.

"He's doing the Russell House Bachelor Auction," Yaya provided helpfully.

"Which I'm in charge of now." *Let's focus on the important things, people.* Imminent career advancement was more important than a deadbeat dad. Though, to be fair, she probably couldn't call him that if he'd never known he had a child.

"Bachelor?" Andie repeated—latching onto the word with a disconcertingly eager gleam in her eyes.

"I have to give Sofie her bath." Rachel stood, unbuckling her daughter—and yes, using her as a human shield against the conversation.

"Apparently he's divorced now," Yaya explained—and Rachel retreated to the bathroom to get Sofie cleaned up and ready for bed with the sound of her mother's glee chasing her down the hall.

Her mother had always been foolishly optimistic when it came to men. She'd believed every lie Rachel's father had ever spun for her—and she seemed well on the way to believing anything Cam wanted to tell her too, without even having met the guy.

Now that he wasn't married anymore, Andie was

undoubtedly conjuring up fantasies of him sweeping Rachel off her feet and straight into a fairy tale happily-ever-after of two-parent family bliss. As if he hadn't lied to her about being married. As if everything was automatically forgiven and the past wouldn't continue to bleed into the future. As if patterns of behavior didn't even exist.

Her mother had never seemed to see the bad things coming—even when they were just natural extensions of everything that had come before. And if Rachel had learned to be extra guarded because her mother had no defenses...well, that wasn't necessarily a bad thing. Sometimes caution was merited—especially when it came to protecting Sofie.

She took her time with the bath time and bed time routines, focusing all her attention on Sofie and trying to push everything else from her mind. These were the moments that mattered—counting and splashing with her daughter in the bath, reading her bedtime stories and singing lullabies. Everything else was secondary—or at least that's what she told herself until Sofie nodded off and she turned on the baby monitor.

She was tempted to simply go to bed early—she was certainly tired enough—but she wouldn't put it past her mother to come wake her up so she could get all the details about Cam.

Dragging her feet, she stepped out of the bedroom to find her mother and Yaya seated around the table, waiting for her. They'd cleaned up the remains of dinner and wiped down the high chair. They sat side-by-side with matching glasses of wine, watching her. Her grandmother's face was expressionless, her eyes calm. Andie's face, on the other hand, was so eager she reminded Rachel of Sofie's jack-in-the-box, coiled and ready to spring. Sofie was terrified of that toy—and looking at her mother, Rachel could definitely empathize.

"Well?" Andie burst as Rachel walked past them to the kitchen to get her own glass.

"The auction is a big event—I'll be working a lot now that it's my responsibility." She poured herself half a glass and screwed the cap back on the bottle. She'd never had much tolerance for alcohol, and nine months without and another year of breastfeeding had turned her into a bona fide lightweight.

Her mother made an impatient noise. Yaya was more direct, her words soft. "Have you decided how you're going to tell him?"

Rachel looked down at the red wine, swirling it in the glass with her back to her mother and grandmother. "What makes you so sure I'm going to tell him?"

"Rachel."

Rachel sighed at the soft, disappointed scold and turned to face them. "Nothing has changed."

"Exactly. You should have told him before," Andie insisted. "Though something *has* changed if he's divorced. I told you that you should have told him. His marriage was obviously already ending. You could have been together all this time."

Rachel took a long drink of wine to stop herself from commenting on exactly how reliable her mother was as a source of advice when it came to men.

"Are you really considering not telling him?" Yaya asked, and the quiet disappointment in the words was like a knife to the stomach.

Yaya had never said what she thought about it one way or the other, but Rachel had always assumed her grandmother was on her side. Yaya'd had a front row seat to the debacle that was Rachel's parents' relationship. She'd picked up the pieces every time Aaron had disappointed Andie and run back home to his wife. Not that Cam was like her father, but Yaya didn't know that. For her to take his side…

It drove home the guilt that had been whispering in the back of Rachel's mind all afternoon. She should have told him. She should have given him the chance to either step up or prove himself as unworthy as her father had been. She'd told herself she was protecting Sofie—before she even knew who Sofie would be—but she'd really been protecting herself. Trying to spare herself the disillusionment.

"He's family," Yaya murmured, the words so soft it was amazing how loudly they echoed in her heart.

Yaya had always wanted a big family. She'd never been shy about admitting that. Her only sister had died when she was a little girl and she'd never wanted her children to go through the loss of their only sibling. But after Andie was born, Rachel's grandfather had gotten cancer for the first time and gone sterile as a result of the treatment. No more children. No big family.

Stavros Persopoulos had lost his third battle with cancer when Andie was fourteen. It seemed to have become a pattern in their family. Little girls without fathers. Women who longed for big families and found themselves raising daughters alone.

Rachel had reached out to her brother when she was pregnant because she wanted her daughter to have family—but she'd denied Sofie the chance to know her father. All because she was scared. Scared because she'd trusted him so much—when she knew better than to trust men. Scared because she'd wanted him so much—when she knew better than to let herself need someone like that. Scared because she knew she would believe him again if he lied—just like her mother had always believed her father. Just like she'd told herself she would never, *ever* do for any man.

But he was family. Sofie's family. And he needed to know the truth.

She sank down at the table, reaching blindly for her mother's and grandmother's hands. "How do I do this?"

CHAPTER SEVEN

Cam straightened the silverware on the white tablecloth for the third time, smiling coolly at the couple at the table next to his and trying to pretend he wasn't as nervous as he'd been when he took Tiffany Williams to the movies when he was fifteen.

Rachel had texted him that morning, asking him to meet her for lunch. Which had to be a positive sign. The last time he'd seen her she'd been spitting fire and telling him to leave the past in the past, but if she wanted to see him now without even the pretext of something to do with the fundraiser, she must have changed her mind—or at least softened toward him a little.

He glanced around the restaurant she'd picked. Classy. Elegant. Not the kind of place you took someone to have a fight. She must be ready to talk. And hopefully ready to listen. They needed to clear the air if they were going to have any hope of moving forward. And he really wanted to move forward.

He hadn't been able to stop thinking about her last night after he left his sister's place. He'd rationalized that maybe it was just pride. Maybe this obsession was born out of the fact that she'd walked away, but it didn't feel like that. It felt like a second chance at something he never should have let slip through his fingers.

He'd been more upset to lose Rachel—a woman he'd known only three weeks—than he had by the combustion of his marriage. He'd told himself at the time that it was only because it took him so off-guard, whereas his divorce had been something they'd been building toward for years, so by the time they agreed to call it quits it was more relief than trauma. But now he wasn't so sure. He seemed to have an unexplored romantic streak because he couldn't stop thinking that running into her again like this was fate.

A throat cleared. "Cam."

She looked stunning, her hair smoothed back into a sleek knot, a blue and green print dress hugging her curves. As composed as always—as long as he didn't notice the strained eyes, tight mouth, and her hands clenched on the purse she held at her waist. Terrified. That's how she looked. Gorgeous and scared out of her friggin' mind. Was the idea of lunch with him really so horrifying?

Cam stood, shoving back his chair. "I was glad to hear from you."

"Well. There are some things we need to discuss."

"Absolutely." *Thank God.* He started to come around the table to hold her chair, but she was already sliding onto the cushion so he returned to his seat. She reached for her water glass, downing half of it—and his spidey-senses twitched. These were not normal nerves. "Is everything all right?"

He started to reach across the table for her hand, but she quickly tucked hers in her lap, her gaze everywhere but on him. *Okay, something's up.* "Rachel?"

"I should have told you before." Her gaze flicked to the table next to them where the couple was completely ignoring them, but her face flamed as if they were eavesdropping. "I didn't think it would be this crowded."

Cam's eyebrows bounced up. The restaurant was half empty, the table on their other side unoccupied, but Rachel clearly wanted privacy. Was that a good thing or a bad thing? "We can go someplace else."

"No, this is good. It's close to..." Her voice trailed off, and for the first time since she'd arrived at the table she met his eyes. "I almost told you by text, but my grandmother said she would disown me if I did."

Told you by text. Echoes of two years ago played in his brain. She'd dumped him by text. Was that what this was? She didn't want him on the Bachelor Auction anymore? She was taking herself off of it because she couldn't stand to be around him? Here he'd been thinking they were clearing the air so they could move forward—was she getting ready to pull the plug?

Cam's hand curled into a fist, but he kept his face devoid of expression.

"I have a daughter."

The words fell in between them and Cam's fist uncurled as surprise made his jaw slack. "What?"

That was the last thing he'd been expecting, but it explained a lot. Why she'd never taken him to her place. Why she'd broken up with him so suddenly.

If she'd been a single mom, worried about introducing him to her daughter, worried about bringing a strange man into her daughter's life and then she'd found out he was married of course she would run without a backward glance.

Relief washed through his chest. Why hadn't she told him before? Had she thought he wouldn't want her when he found out she had a kid? He loved kids. He wanted kids. He actually *liked* the idea of a woman who already had one, but he wasn't sure they'd ever talked about that kind of thing during their whirlwind three weeks together. It all made sense. Cam felt his lips start to curl. This was good—

"Her name is Sofie and she's eighteen months old."

He blinked. That was younger than he'd thought. She must have been—

His mind went blank as the significance of the math thundered through him. *Eighteen months, plus nine months…*

September.

He knew before she said the words.

"She's yours."

*****

Cam didn't look like he was taking it well.

Though she wasn't sure how she'd expected him to take it. Pure, glazed, unvarnished shock wasn't the *best* response, but it wasn't the worst either.

"We have a child," he said finally, his deep voice deceptively calm.

"A daughter. Sofia."

"Where is she?" His gaze flicked around the restaurant as if Sofie might jump out from beneath a table and yell surprise.

"I didn't bring her."

Cam's eyes locked on hers, his gaze darkening as his jaw clenched. "You didn't trust me."

It was a statement, not a question, but she explained anyway. "I didn't know how you would react. I have pictures." She scrambled for her phone, fumbling it out of her purse.

"What did you think I would do?" He shook his head sharply. "Don't answer that."

"I have to think of her first." She could see his anger

building and the situation slipping farther and farther from her grasp. As a peace offering, she pulled up her lock screen—an image of Sofie at the playground—and turned her phone toward him. His eyes locked on the image, something in his expression going still as she whispered, "I thought you might be upset—"

"Because you kept her from me for two years?"

His voice seemed to echo and Rachel glanced nervously at the table beside them—the couple there had been ignoring them earlier, but they definitely had their attention now. She pitched her own voice low. "You were married."

"So that justified it." He tore his gaze off the phone and his grey eyes seemed nearly black as they met hers. "Would you ever have told me, if we hadn't run into each other yesterday?"

She opened her mouth, but there weren't any words to make this better. Because she might not have. She might have left him in ignorance for his entire life. Or at least until Sofie was old enough to make her own choice whether or not her father was in her life. The screen in her hands went dark.

"I have to think of Sofie," she whispered, unable to meet his eyes. "I want her to have everything I never did."

"Like a father?"

She flinched.

They'd never fought before—in the dizzy first flush of those three weeks everything had been perfect and then she'd broken things off without giving him the option. She was unprepared for him to lash out like a wounded bear—and unprepared for him to know exactly which barbs to throw at her. Suddenly she wished he didn't know her so well. That she hadn't been so open with him about her past back then. That she hadn't trusted him so much. He knew everything.

She met his eyes, her skin cold and her face calm. "I hate that I was honest with you when you were lying to me."

"I wasn't lying," he growled, leaning across the table. "I was waiting for the right moment, trying to find a way to tell you in a way you'd understand."

"Then you should be able to understand why I didn't tell you about Sofie."

"You were just waiting for the right moment?" He rocked back in his chair, sarcasm heavy in his voice. He shook his head, disgusted. "I had a right to know."

"Why?" she demanded, defensiveness that he was right making her voice sharp. "Because you provided the genetic material?"

"We were more than that."

"Were we? I can't remember."

Except she could. Even having all those memories tainted by the belief that he'd cast her as his mistress hadn't completely erased them. She remembered what it felt like when they'd been together. The possibility. The hope. The rightness of it.

Cam was staring down at the table cloth, his hands flat on the table, breathing slowly in and out like he was trying to force himself to calm. He had a level-headed reputation. The catcher who could calm down any pitcher and stop a bench-clearing brawl before it could start. That reputation was being put to the test today.

Finally he looked up, a man wearing his calm like an ill-fitting Halloween mask. His gaze flicked down to the darkened phone. "Can I meet her?"

Rachel's stomach dipped and swung. She'd been expecting those words, but still they caught her right in the gut. "Of course." She swallowed down her nerves, clenching both hands around her phone. "That's why I picked this place. It's close to my apartment. We can go there after we eat."

"Let's go now." He shoved back his chair, already pulling a twenty from his wallet and dropping it on the white tablecloth even though they hadn't ordered anything.

She wanted to argue, to delay, to come up with some excuse—but there wasn't any. Cam wanted to meet his daughter. However he felt right now, she knew he would never hurt Sofie—and he wasn't likely to calm down and enjoy a pleasant lunch with Rachel before he saw her.

She pushed back her chair. "You can follow me in your car."

* * * * *

He had a daughter. A daughter. The words kept repeating inside him, like they were rewriting his DNA with the new knowledge that he was a father.

Cam flexed his hands on the steering wheel and concentrated on following Rachel's car down the quiet city streets. Not too close—he didn't want her to accuse him of tailgating—but close enough that no other cars could get between them. On his way to meet his daughter.

He'd always wanted to be a dad.

Well. Maybe not always. He hadn't really given it much thought until the last few years when it had become a point of contention with Erika and he'd realized it wasn't something he was willing to give up on. He loved his nieces and nephews, loved being the fun uncle, but he also wanted more. He wanted the whole shebang—first steps, dirty diapers, skinned knees. He wanted to be the one they ran to when they were upset. He wanted to be the one to put the fear of God into any potential boyfriends so they wouldn't dream of hurting his baby.

He *wanted* that. And it was hard not to be pissed at Rachel for depriving him of the time he could have already spent with his daughter. Sofia. He hadn't even gotten to name her. Or even *consult* on the name.

He knew Rachel had been upset when she thought he was married and he understood that, but how could she not tell him? That didn't even seem to be on the same *scale*. This was his *child*.

They pulled into the parking lot of a modest, low-rise apartment complex and Cam followed Rachel to the lot alongside one of the buildings. He shut off the engine and closed his eyes, pulling hard on his calm. No matter how he felt about Rachel right now—and he had several choice words he would undoubtedly be sharing with her later—his daughter wasn't part of that. He needed to make the best possible first impression. Even if she might not remember this, he would remember it for the rest of his life.

He opened his eyes and stepped out of the car. Rachel was waiting for him on the sidewalk. She didn't say a word, turning toward the exterior staircase as he fell into step behind her.

It had warmed up overnight and yesterday's snow was already melting, dripping off the eaves in a steady rhythm that seemed unnaturally loud, as did their footsteps as they clomped up the stairs. Her keys jingled as she unlocked the door and she called out, "Yaya, we're here," as she pushed it open—

And then he was stepping into the apartment, looking around, his eyes landing on his child. His daughter.

She stood on pudgy legs in the middle of a cordoned off play area, clutching an oversized Elmo stuffed animal in one arm and an empty Kleenex box in the other. He'd seen the picture, but somehow hadn't been able to wrap his head around it. She hadn't been real until this moment, and he realized as he stood there that she was bigger than he'd expected. Taller. With more curly dark hair flying in every direction. There was an older woman in the room as well, but he couldn't take his eyes off the baby long enough to greet her. His daughter lifted her soft baby face toward the door, instantly dropping both items she held and thrusting her arms into the air. "Mama! Up!"

"Hi, sweet girl." Rachel set down her bag and walked to the play area.

"Up!" The toddler demanded again, arms thrust imperiously upward, and Rachel reached over the barrier surrounding the play area and lifted her into her arms.

Mother and child turned toward him. And suddenly he couldn't breathe.

CHAPTER EIGHT

Cam didn't look so good.

He'd gone pale, standing woodenly in the doorway, his eyes never leaving Sofie. Her daughter's warm weight was a comfort in her arms as she faced him, her own nerves oddly calmed by seeing him so overwhelmed.

"This is Sofie," she explained unnecessarily. "Sofie, this is Cam."

That got a reaction. He shot her a look and Rachel flushed.

"Your daddy," she amended awkwardly—not that Sofie would understand. The words were for Cam. Sofie didn't entirely understand the concept of parents yet. There were just people in her life who adored her. Whether they were called Mama or Yaya or Gam—as she called her grandmother—they were just satellites orbiting her, the star at the center of their world.

"Hello, Sofie," Cam said softly, his scratchy voice sounding even deeper and raspier than usual. "It's nice to meet you."

Sofie stared at Cam in silence, studying him, until he took a step toward them. Sofie turned her head away sharply, burying her face in Rachel's shoulder, her little arms suddenly clinging tight as if to make sure Rachel wasn't considering handing her to the strange man.

Sofie was usually social, smiling and waving at everyone she met, but she must have been picking up on Rachel's tension. She soothed the baby with a soft sound and a hand on her back. "It's okay, Sofie Bear," she murmured.

Though nothing felt okay.

She didn't know what to do. Cam stared at Sofie. Sofie cowered from Cam. Yaya watched it all. And Rachel had no freaking idea what she was supposed to do next. She'd thought about what she would say to him, how she would tell him. She'd thought about the moment when he would see his daughter. She just hadn't let herself think beyond that and now panic was starting to claw up into her chest.

"Maybe you should go."

Cam jolted like she'd tazed him. "What?"

"You can come back later. It's almost time for her nap." It was true but it was an excuse. A desperate excuse. "I just think we could all use some time to process. We can talk again in a day or two. Figure out…figure out what's next…"

"Rachel." He stepped forward, as if he might reach for Sofie, but the baby was still clinging to her, refusing to look up. For a moment she thought he might argue. Refuse to go. Part of her almost wanted him to—though she wasn't sure whether it was because she wanted him to take charge of the situation or because she wanted him to be unreasonable so she could dislike him and feel less like the villain in the room.

His expression was so raw when he looked at Sofie. So vulnerable. And Rachel was starting to realize he might not be the guy she'd told herself he was for the last two years.

But that still didn't mean she knew what to do with him.

"Okay," he said finally. His right hand flexed at his side. "If that's what you want."

She didn't know what she wanted, but she nodded as if she did, shifting Sofie in her arms.

Cam nodded as well, his Adam's apple shifting as he swallowed. "Okay," he repeated. Sofie had lifted her head and was now peering at him curiously. His gaze fell back to her and didn't move, like he was trying to memorize her face.

Rachel let him stare until she couldn't stand the awkwardness anymore. She cleared her throat and Cam jerked.

"I'll see you soon." He moved quickly once he started, out the door, his footsteps receding down the steps outside.

Rachel hugged Sofie, breathing in her sweet baby scent and hoping she hadn't made a huge mistake.

*****

"What do you mean you have a daughter? Like, a *daughter* daughter?" Shelby demanded.

"Is there another definition for that word?" Carly snapped at their sister, so at least Cam didn't have to.

He'd driven straight to Carly's house after Rachel kicked him out. He'd wanted to argue. Wanted to stay. Wanted to hold his child. But he didn't know what to do, so he'd honored her wishes and left—hoping as he did so that he was somehow proving she could trust him. If she knew he would leave when she asked, wouldn't she be more likely to let him back in? He needed to be let back in. That was his daughter. His baby.

"Yes, a daughter daughter. Her name is Sofia and she's a year and a half old."

Shelby swore softly under her breath and Cam

silently echoed the sentiment. This wasn't at all what he'd expected when he went to meet Rachel for lunch. He never would have thought he could feel this desperate—or this angry at her.

She'd kept him from his child. Maybe it was a good thing he'd left her apartment. He'd been so focused on Sofie that he hadn't acknowledged the anger simmering beneath the surface toward her mother, but it was there, bubbling hotter every time he thought about the two years he'd lost.

First words. First steps. So many milestones.

"Are you sure it's yours?" Shelby asked—and everyone in the room turned to glare at her.

He'd driven to Carly's without calling or texting ahead, not thinking—hoping his sister would be home and not out Christmas shopping on a Saturday afternoon less than three weeks from Christmas. He'd found not just Carly, but Shelby and Ashley as well. They'd been baking cookies for a school fundraiser—a task which had been delegated to the husbands as soon as Carly had seen Cam's face. They were now cloistered in her upstairs "sewing room"—which, to Cam's knowledge, had never actually been used for sewing and was actually where she went when she needed to close a door between her and her passel of children.

Children she'd been there for the birth of—though that was stupid. Of course she had. She'd given birth to them. But his brain wasn't working. All he could seem to think of was all the things he'd missed because Rachel had decided he was evil. He hadn't been there when his own baby was born.

"What?" Shelby demanded when Ashley and Carly turned death glares on her. "It's a valid question. He's a professional athlete."

"She's mine."

"I'm just saying, a little paternity test goes a long way—"

"Shelby. She's mine." And he hadn't even gotten a picture of her. Shit. Why hadn't he taken a picture?

"Okay." Carly clasped her hands, leaning forward. "Next steps. What's the situation? What's the relationship with the mom? Obviously you knew her."

"We dated a couple years ago. It was before my divorce with Erika was final and when she found out I was still technically married she assumed the worst. Instead of talking to me, she broke up with me via text and I never heard from her again until this week. She's coordinating the Russell House fundraiser."

"The Bachelor Auction?" Ashley perked up. "She picked you for a bachelor auction?"

"She didn't pick me. Don't look so excited. It wasn't a ploy to see me again. She had no idea I was involved when her boss assigned her to the event."

"That you know of."

"She kept the existence of my child from me for *years,*" he reminded Ashley.

"Okay, but maybe she *wanted* to tell you."

"Ashley," Carly cut in. "Not helping."

Cam wasn't sure what would help at the moment. He didn't know why he'd come. He'd somehow thought that Carly, who always thought she knew what was best for everyone, would know what to do.

"I take it you want to be in her life," Carly said.

"Of course I do."

She nodded. "Good. Knowing what you want is the first step. Now we just have to figure out how to get it."

"She wouldn't have told you unless she wanted you in the baby's life," Ashley said.

"Or money," Shelby added.

Carly shot the younger two a look to shut them up, but Cam frowned. Why *had* she told him? He'd been so focused on the fact that she'd kept the secret for so long that he'd never really thought of why she'd changed her mind.

She knew he wasn't married anymore. She knew he hadn't used her the way she'd assumed. But she'd still been so guarded. So protective of the baby, holding her like she was afraid Cam would snatch her out of her arms.

But she had told him.

There had to be a reason. Maybe they could start with that. He still wanted to roar when he thought about what she'd done, but maybe he needed to stop thinking about all he'd missed so he didn't miss out on any more.

Carly smiled, seeing the shift in his expression. "Ready to look forward?"

He narrowed his eyes. "You know it's really annoying how you think you're right all the time."

"You love that I'm right all the time. That's why you came to me. You needed someone to tell you to stop dwelling on pointless shit in the past that you can't change and focus on the baby and the future. Say, *Thank you, Carly.*"

"Please don't," Ashley begged. "She's insufferable enough as it is."

"Have you noticed her ego just keeps getting bigger?" Shelby commented. "You'd think it would have a maximum size, but no."

"You'd all be lost without me," Carly declared, her ego on full display. "And I expect gratitude in the form of lavish, over-the-top Christmas presents."

"That reminds me," Ashley said sweetly, "I need to

get to the Dollar Store to finish my Christmas shopping."

As his sisters continued bickering cheerfully amongst themselves, Cam let the sound wash over him, calming his anxiety. Sofia was family. Rachel was family now. And family made it work. He was going to be part of their lives. They were going to make it work.

*****

Three hours later, Rachel still had no idea how this was going to work. She'd gone over every moment of the aborted lunch and Cam's introduction to Sofie, and she couldn't seem to get the look on his face when he'd looked at their daughter out of her head—the combination of shock and wonder and vulnerability, like his entire heart had been laid out for her to see.

It was exactly how she felt every time she looked at Sofie. And it scared the crap out of her.

Somehow this would be so much easier if he hadn't looked at her daughter like she'd taken his whole heart at first glance.

Her mother and Yaya had taken Sofie to the grocery store so Rachel could think, since riding in the cart and waving at people was one of the baby's favorite pastimes. Rachel knew if she stayed in the apartment she'd only drive herself crazy. She had to do something productive, so she grabbed her car keys and headed to the storage locker to collect the Christmas stuff she'd been neglecting for the last week and a half.

She'd just punched in the code for the storage place's gate when her phone rang. Panic stabbed in her chest and she *knew* it was Cam. The number wasn't one she recognized. A seven-two-oh area code. Her rational brain argued that it could be any local caller, but her heart wasn't listening. She hit the button to connect the call, her pulse thundering in her ears, and the SUV jerked through the opening gate as she stomped on the gas a little too hard.

"Hello?" she asked breathlessly.

"Rachel."

Cam's distinctive voice rasped through the speakers and she shivered, pulling into the parking spot in front of her storage locker. "Cam."

"I know you said we'd talk in a couple days, but I couldn't wait."

"No, this is good," she assured him, trying to convince herself at the same time. "I was making myself nuts wondering…"

"I want to be part of her life, Rache."

She closed her eyes against the sincerity—and the nickname. "I know," she whispered. But that was a thousand times scarier than if he'd wanted nothing to do with them. She couldn't deny him access, but she was so freaking scared to trust him. Sofie was her everything.

"So what are we going to do?" she said, louder, since he could probably barely hear her through the car's sound system.

"It's all about her now," he said. "So we make it work. I'd like to see her again, as soon as possible. And I want her to meet my family. You both should. Maybe just a few of them to start, but we have a lot of Christmas gatherings and I'd love for her to get to know her cousins. Maybe even bring her to Christmas Eve dinner—"

"Cam." Her heartbeat was too loud again, the momentum of his words scaring her senseless. It was too much too fast.

"Sorry," he rasped. "One thing at a time?"

"Yeah," she murmured.

Of course he would want to take Sofie places—but even the thought of her baby going to an innocuous holiday gathering was pushing her panic button. It wasn't that she didn't trust Cam with Sofie, but she just...if he took her, she wouldn't know where she was. She *always* knew where Sofie was. Even when she was with her mom or Yaya. She couldn't exactly fit Sofie with a tracking device every time she handed her over to Cam—though if someone hadn't already invented Baby Lo-Jack, they really should.

But he was right. They had to start somewhere. And the sooner the better since she knew she'd only make herself sick with dread until he saw Sofie again.

Her gaze landed on the storage locker in front of her. "We were going to put up a Christmas tree with Sofie tonight. If you want to come by and..."

"I'd love that," he answered, before she could figure out what the *and* might be.

"Good." Rachel nodded, even though he couldn't see her. Her gaze flicked to the console and the unfamiliar number there. "Is this your new number?"

"It's my sister's," he admitted after a slight hesitation. "I wasn't sure if you'd still blocked mine."

She cringed. Because she had still blocked his number. "I'll unblock it," she promised. "Do you want to come by after dinner? Say six-thirty or seven? We eat pretty early with Sofie."

"Sure. I'll see you then."

"Great," she mumbled, already regretting the invitation—but Cam was saying goodbye and disconnecting the call and all she could do was load the Christmas decorations into her car and hope for the best.

CHAPTER NINE

The man was amazing with Sofie.

Patient. Encouraging. Goofy enough to make her giggle.

Rachel watched as Cam lifted Sofie up to place an ornament on the tree and had to resist the urge to snatch her daughter out of his arms. Not because he was doing anything wrong, but because he was doing it so effortlessly right. And it was driving her a little crazy.

The image of Cam she'd built in her head since finding out he was married was of a selfish player. The kind of man who could never put another person's need above his own. The kind of man who was disgusted by diapers and snot and always a little awkward with children.

This Cam was nothing like that.

He was gentle and sweet, and so careful with Sofie that Rachel couldn't even be annoyed with him. He was a freaking natural—and instead of being grateful, she couldn't stop being jealous that Sofie had taken to him so completely. She was giggling and clapping and declaring, "Nen!"—her version of *again*—every time they hung another ornament in the wrong place on the tree.

They were doing it all wrong—and it was taking all of Rachel's willpower not to say anything. She'd been putting this tree up for the last ten years and she knew the ornaments, knew exactly where they needed to go so the most special ones were on clear display and everything was perfectly spaced. There was a system. And Cam and Sofie were blowing that system to hell, giggling all the way.

It was unsettling, the wrongness scraping along her nerves like sandpaper.

Though it was possible it was guilt and jealousy making her feel like an exposed wire on a faulty strand of Christmas lights. Guilt that she might have been so wrong about him and jealousy that it all seemed to come so easily to him.

He'd already completely charmed her mother and grandmother—which really shouldn't have been possible. They were supposed to be on her side, and providing a buffer between her and Cam. She'd worried they would be bothered that she'd invited Cam to invade their family time. They always put up the tree together. But barely ten minutes after Cam arrived her mother declared that they were out of tinsel and couldn't possibly put the tree up without it. Before Rachel could argue that they forgot the tinsel half the time anyway, Andie had rushed off to the store to get some.

Rachel hadn't been suspicious until Yaya had decreed that decorating the tree required cocoa and defected to the kitchen to unearth the perfect cocoa recipe she was sure she'd hidden there somewhere. The apartment was small enough that Yaya could probably still hear every word they said in the living room, but she was too far away for Rachel to use her as a human shield and Rachel was starting to suspect her mother and grandmother had conspired to give her time alone with Cam and Sofie.

Which wasn't what she'd had in mind at all. She'd wanted to get to know him again at a safe distance. Let him into their life bit by bit.

And yes, a small, petty part of her had wanted him to be on the outside, had wanted him to see that Sofie had a great family without him and that none of them needed him.

This was better, obviously. It was better for Sofie if he fit right into their family like a missing puzzle piece. But it was making her feel a little unhinged and she was selfishly regretting inviting him to come tonight.

Especially when Cam and Sofie picked up the godawful ugly Elvis Santa ornament and put it right front and center.

She'd promised herself she wasn't going to comment on the ornaments that were out of place—she could just fix them later—but when Cam turned away from the tree with Sofie in his arms, he caught her watching him.

His smile shifted, becoming less generally happy and more specifically aimed at her, and taking on a teasing edge, as if he could sense how much the haphazard ornament placement was bothering her. His eyes crinkled at the edges, a knowing light appearing in them—and Rachel was suddenly, viscerally reminded of how it had felt to have him smile at her like that. As if they had a secret, and the secret was how crazy he was about her.

Her breath quickened, her knees wobbling at the sight of this man holding her daughter in the crook of his arm so naturally—until she forcibly squashed the little whisper of chemistry trying to take hold. Things were already complicated enough without her remembering why she was attracted to him.

Rachel turned away, her glance catching on the clock which was—thank God—already showing seven forty-five. "I should get Sofie ready for bed. If she stays up too late it upsets her whole schedule."

"Can I help?"

She turned back, ready to tell him that wouldn't be necessary, ready to bristle and remind him that she'd been doing it on her own for the last year and a half—but the expression on his face stopped her.

It was cautious. Earnest. He stood there, beside the Christmas tree, cuddling their daughter in his arms, looking like he wasn't ready for her to be taken away, and Rachel's heart melted a little around the frostiest edges.

"Please?" he added.

She couldn't say no. Damn it.

Rachel pressed her lips together and nodded without a word. Cam's face lit and she swallowed hard before calling to Yaya that they were putting Sofie to bed. "Bath time, baby!" she told her daughter, pointedly not looking at the man holding her.

Sofie threw out her arms and lunged from Cam's arms into Rachel's. She caught the baby's solid weight, relieved that Sofie wasn't resisting bedtime. The last thing she needed was Cam watching and judging as she had to deal with a toddler tantrum.

She led the way into the bedroom she shared with Sofie. Self-consciousness swamped her as she tried not to look at the double bed, or the hamper overflowing with laundry. She didn't know which made this experience more awkward—the awareness she had of him as a man, or the anxiety that he was watching and judging her every move as a mother.

She'd never had him in her space before, back in that

stupid September. She'd always met him at restaurants or at his place, hyperaware of the stark difference between their lifestyles. Her little one bedroom apartment had hardly been able to compare to his sprawling four-thousand square foot luxury condo.

Did he still have that condo? He must have sold it when he moved to LA. Though wherever he was staying now was undoubtedly equally luxurious.

He didn't belong here, taking up too much space in her cramped little bedroom with her Target furniture.

She grabbed a set of rainbow footie pajamas and a fresh diaper from the drawers beneath the changing table and carried them into the attached bathroom, Cam trailing behind her, his sheer bulk making him impossible to ignore.

"What can I do?" he asked.

It was automatic to say *nothing,* but she caught the word before it could get out. "Run water for the bath while I get her ready?"

Cam nodded instantly, moving toward the tub. He picked up the pink Sesame Street bubble bath. "Bubbles?"

"Bub!" Sofie declared enthusiastically.

"Um, just a few. She loves them, but she tries to eat them."

"Do you do that?" Cam asked Sofie with a grin. "My mom said I used to try to eat dish soap. I guess you come by it naturally."

The reality hit Rachel in that moment. While talking about her baby eating soap of all things, the realization shuddered through her that this wasn't just one night to get through.

Cam was Sofie's father. His genes were the reason she tried to eat soap. And he wasn't going anywhere.

Unless he got bored with the whole fatherhood thing—but that didn't seem like Cam. Not with the way he was looking at Sofie like everything she did was magical.

Rachel focused on the baby, trying to ignore the panic rabbits now ricocheting around the inside of her brain.

The bathwater was the perfect depth and temperature, with the perfect amount of bubbles. Because of course he was effortlessly perfect.

"Is it all right?" Cam asked as she tested it and Rachel's chest tightened at the look in his eyes—as if getting the bathwater right was the most important thing in the world at that moment.

"It's great," she murmured, her voice unaccountably choked. She cleared her throat, lifting Sofie into the tub.

"Bob!" she squealed, slapping her hands on the water and instantly lifting the bubbles that clung to her fingers to her mouth.

"Do you want to get Bob the Duck?" Rachel nodded toward the bath toy and Cam grinned.

"Bob?" he asked as he reached for the bright blue rubber duck. He crouched down beside her at the edge of the tub, extending the toy.

"He bobs," Rachel explained, blushing as their shoulders brushed. Sofie smacked Bob beneath the surface, watching him bob up. She ran the washcloth over the baby's shoulders as Cam continued to entertain Sofie, making sound effects as he motored Bob around the bathwater. Like a freaking natural. "Where did you get so good with kids?"

"Lots of nieces and nephews," Cam explained, in between motorboat noises. "I have three sisters. All with kids."

Rachel tried to smother the self-consciousness that

rose up as she rinsed Sofie and lifted her out of the bath and swathed her in a towel. "Do you want to…?" She nodded toward the pajamas and the diaper she'd laid out.

"Yeah?" Cam beamed as if she'd just offered him a winning lottery ticket and reached for Sofie. "Come here, sweet girl."

Rachel hadn't known anything about kids before Sofie was born. She'd had to figure everything out as she went, with her mother, Yaya, and Google as her only advisors. Of course Cam was comfortable with Sofie. He'd had practice.

She hadn't realized how badly she wanted him to flail nervously like she had at first until he made it look so damn easy, putting Sofie's fresh diaper on her and fitting her squirming limbs into the pajamas like he'd done it a thousand times.

The man was freaking Super Dad. And it was giving her a complex.

She hadn't been prepared for Cam to swoop back into her life. Hadn't been prepared for him to be anything other than the villain she'd cast him as in her mind in self-defense for the last two years. And she certainly hadn't been prepared for him to actually want to be a dad. And not just the kind of dad who played with the kids and then handed them back to Mom. The kind of dad who wanted to do bath time and bed time.

Though maybe once the novelty wore off he wouldn't anymore. But what if this really was the kind of relationship he wanted? Could she trust it? Could she trust him?

She'd done that once before. She'd stepped outside of her usual cautious comfort zone and believed in him—and he'd been married the entire time. Even if he had been getting a divorce, even if there had been extenuating circumstances, he should have told her. Maybe she wouldn't have taken it well, but it couldn't have been any worse than being blindsided like she had been.

Maybe she should have let him explain—but how many times had her father talked his way back into her mother's good graces? Cam was charming—and she hadn't wanted to be her mother.

But now…were things different? Did he really want to be a dad?

She wasn't ready for any of this. The Wonder Dad routine was too good to be true. And she was braced for the other shoe to drop.

CHAPTER TEN

Cam stared in the bathroom mirror and silently commanded himself to get his shit together. All night he'd felt like his world was breaking apart and reshaping with a new center. It wasn't theoretical anymore. He was a father. And he didn't know what the hell he was doing.

He didn't know the baby's routine. He hadn't known which bedtime story was her favorite. Or what the name of her favorite bath toy was. Or which stuffed animal she needed to kiss on the nose before she would go to sleep.

He didn't know any of those things about his nieces or nephews either. He hadn't needed to in order to be a good uncle, but this was different. This wasn't uncle territory. This was daddy territory and he was hopelessly out of his depth.

Rachel was a good mom. He'd never known this side of her, and he was starting to think they hadn't really known one another at all. They'd just enjoyed one another, playing together. Sure, they'd had a few serious conversations—enough that he felt like he understood her, understood why she was such a planner—but there were so many things they didn't know about one another. He'd always thought there would be more time for the serious stuff. And then she'd been gone. And now the serious stuff was here without warning.

This was a whole new ball game. She was a mom. He was trying to figure out how to be a dad. And neither of them seemed to know how to talk to one another.

Cam washed his hands and splashed cold water on his face, hoping to clear his head. He'd retreated to the bathroom after Sofie had fallen asleep in her crib—in part to gather his thoughts, but also in an attempt to keep Rachel from instantly kicking him out now that his excuse for being here was asleep. They still had so much to say to one another, though he had no idea where to start.

He wasn't ready for any of this. But sometimes your shot at the majors came before you were ready for it and you had to play your best and hope that it was enough to keep you in the game...and not psych yourself out and ruin your hope of ever getting another shot again if you got kicked back down to the minors. He'd perfected the art of projecting confidence and pretending he had it all under control.

"You've got this," he reminded his reflection—and headed back out into the living room.

The apartment was tiny. It was hard to imagine three adults and a toddler all lived here. The space probably would have felt even more claustrophobic if it hadn't been so ruthlessly organized. There was a place for everything—and he could see Rachel's influence in every tidy little shelf and cubby.

When he came back into the living room, the doors to the other bedrooms were conspicuously closed and Rachel's mother and grandmother had made themselves scarce again. Rachel was standing at the tree, putting up the last ornaments. Or, to be more accurate, fixing them. As he watched, she plucked an ornament he'd put up off the tree and moved it to a lower branch, her movements quick and sure.

Cam suppressed a smile. It had been driving her crazy earlier, watching him haphazardly hang ornaments all over her tree. He was amazed she'd managed to restrain herself from fixing them this long. She moved two more ornaments and took a step back to study her work.

"Better?"

She jumped and whirled toward him, a rosy glow rising to her cheeks. "Sorry, I just…"

"Couldn't stand it anymore?" He smiled and she took another step away from the tree, as if to stop herself from continuing to tweak it.

"I wanted to tell you I'm sorry," she said suddenly, and he thought she meant about moving the ornaments until she continued. "For not telling you before. Though if you'd told me the truth about your marital status—" She bit off the words. "Anyway I'm sorry."

"So am I. For not telling you about Erika. I wanted to—"

She shook her head, interrupting, "We need to move past that. For Sofie."

"For Sofie," he conceded, though he didn't want it to just be for Sofie.

"My brother offered to kick your ass. I almost let him, but in retrospect I'm glad I didn't."

Cam frowned. "I thought you weren't in touch with him."

"I wasn't. I, uh, got in touch after…"

After they broke up. After she found out about Sofie. He wanted to ask her when she'd realized she was pregnant. If she'd been excited or scared. Why she hadn't called him. But he didn't want to push his luck.

He nodded to the tree to distract her before she could decide they were done and kick him out. "Do you always use a fake tree?"

She glanced toward it. "It isn't fake. It's still a Christmas tree. It's just..."

"Not alive?"

"It's easier. And cheaper. Do you know how expensive live trees are? And then you just throw them away in a month."

"I'm happy to help out with money. And I don't just mean the tree." Cam glanced around the tiny apartment. It was cozy. Homey and comfortable. But kids were expensive. He'd heard his sisters bemoaning that often enough.

She bristled, pursing her lips. "We're doing fine. Thanks." She turned back to the tree, dismissing the subject and continuing to adjust ornaments.

"Do you have a schematic in your head of where each ornament goes?"

From her profile he could see her mouth tighten even more. "I just want it to be perfect. It's the first Christmas tree Sofie might remember."

At one and a half? "I'm pretty sure she isn't going to know the difference."

"I know that. But I still want it to be perfect."

Perfect to him had always been an illusion. He and Erika had the perfect marriage—and it had vanished like smoke. He had the perfect career—and it felt like he was hanging on by his fingernails. Perfect was an impossible standard, an appearance to keep up. And sometimes he was exhausted just thinking about it.

"Perfect is overrated," he murmured. "Sometimes the imperfections are the best part." He closed the distance between them, eyeing the flawlessly symmetrical tree and the woman working so hard to make everything perfect.

Rachel was a planner, he knew that, but if life always went exactly to plan, he would still be married to Erika. He wouldn't have met Rachel and they wouldn't have Sofie. Sometimes the accidents life handed them when they were striving for perfection were the best opportunities. A wild pitch that turned into a double play to get them out of an inning. Or a checked swing that turned into a game winning base hit. He'd learned to roll with what the universe handed him—and right now it seemed to be handing him a second chance with Rachel.

The anger he'd felt this afternoon had already bled away, leaving the memory of what he'd wanted them to be in its place. He'd never been good at holding grudges. One of the most critical tools a ball player could have was a short memory—the ability to forget the mistakes of the past and focus on the next pitch, rather than the one he'd just missed. Cam hadn't always been able to do that—every player went through phases where he got in his head—but he was determined not to strike out this time.

The light of the Christmas tree glowed on the side of her face and reflected in her eyes. Eyes that locked on his as the moment held, lingering.

"Rachel," he murmured, reaching to tuck a lock of hair behind her ear.

She ducked her head, tucking the hair back herself, and her gaze flicked away from his. "Sofie's asleep now. Maybe you should..."

Cam dropped his hand, reading the rejection loud and clear. He thrust his hands into his pockets, rocking back. "I'd like you and Sofie to meet my family. Maybe this week sometime?"

"Of course." Rachel nodded, still not meeting his eyes. "I'll look at my schedule and we'll work something out."

"Good." He searched his brain for something else to say, some other way to put off leaving. There was nowhere else in the world he wanted to be right now. Sofie was asleep, but she was here. Rachel was pushing him away, but she was here.

But he didn't want Rachel to regret inviting him over. He didn't want her to think twice about doing it again because she worried she couldn't get rid of him. So it was time to leave gracefully, even if it felt wrong to walk away.

"I'll see you soon," he promised as Rachel watched him put on his shoes and coat from a safe distance, her arms folded across her middle. "Thank you for tonight."

* * * * *

Rachel closed the door behind Cam, locking the deadbolt and resting her forehead against the smooth, cold surface.

"Oh! Did Cameron leave already?"

Rachel barely resisted the urge to roll her eyes at her mother's badly feigned surprise. "You know he did."

Her mother must have been eavesdropping to come out so soon after Cam's departure—not that she could blame her. The apartment's thin walls weren't exactly the height of noise insulation. Until they'd gotten Sofie a white noise machine, she'd been waking up every time someone spoke above a whisper in the living room.

"He seems like a nice boy."

Cam was hardly a boy. He was a man—and that was half the problem. It would have been easy to resist a boy who wasn't ready for the reality of having a kid. It would have been easy to dismiss him and get back to her regularly scheduled life.

Restraining her comment since she *really* didn't want to get into a whole post-mortem of Cam's visit, Rachel pushed off the door, her limbs suddenly heavy with exhaustion. She moved past her mother into the kitchen, automatically going through the routine of tidying up and getting ready for tomorrow.

Her mother didn't take the hint, following her into the kitchen. "Sofie seems to like him. Babies have good instincts."

Rachel cringed at that glimpse into her mother's decision making process. No wonder she blindly trusted everyone she met. Rachel couldn't afford to do that. She needed to be smart. It was her job to look out for Sofie. To be the suspicious one so Sofie didn't have to. She couldn't afford to let her guard down around Cam.

Even if part of her wanted to.

There had been a moment by the tree. Intimate. Humming with possibility. Reminding her of the time when she'd thought he was a good guy. When she'd trusted him. When she'd wanted to give him her whole heart.

She couldn't afford moments like those. Right now she had enough to manage just trying to navigate this new situation.

Everything was going to change.

It had been the right thing to do, telling him. She knew that, but she still wished she hadn't had to. She'd liked her life. She'd been in control of her life, but now…everything was spiraling out of control and she'd never liked that feeling.

Her mother's arm slid around her waist from the side. "Everything's going to work out."

"You don't know that," she mumbled.

"I do," Andie insisted.

Rachel shook her head, resisting the comfort. Because she knew how empty that comfort was. Words with nothing behind them. Her mother believed everything would work out—but never did anything to *make* it work. Rachel had learned early that if she wanted something to happen, she had to do it herself.

And that she should never trust her mother's judgment.

Andie trusted too much, too easily, and Rachel wasn't going to make that mistake. Not again.

CHAPTER ELEVEN

The house was huge. Rachel stared up at it nervously, adjusting Sofie in her arms.

Cam had told her they were meeting at his sister's place. The gathering tonight was supposed to be only his sisters and his parents—the spouses were taking all Cam's nieces and nephews to the movies so she and Sofie wouldn't be bombarded by the entire family at once. His grandmother lived with his parents, but she was apparently easily confused and had stayed home to watch *The Great British Bake Off* since Cam wanted to keep this first meeting small. Just his parents and sisters—but there were still four SUVs crowding into the driveway in front of hers, each one a more expensive brand than the last. BMW. Porsche. Land Rover. Apparently that was the stratosphere Cam's family lived in. Unless he'd bought them all cars when he signed his free-agent contract.

Was Cam the kind of guy who gave his family extravagant presents? He'd flown Rachel to San Francisco for the weekend to see him play and given her a jersey to wear to the game that she'd later found out was worth hundreds—a jersey that was still hidden in the back of her closet—but she hadn't thought anything of the gifts at the time. Now as she carried her daughter past the row of eighty-thousand dollar cars, she saw those memories in a new light.

Would he want to give Sofie expensive gifts? Cell phones and iPads and a car on her sixteenth birthday? She knew she was getting ahead of herself, borrowing trouble from a future that might never come, but she couldn't seem to stop the agitated spiral of her thoughts. She was too nervous, those panic-bunnies bouncing in her brain.

She didn't feel ready for this, meeting Cam's family—though it was better than seeing him alone again. She'd thrown herself into her work over the last few days, focusing on preparations for the Bachelor Auction, but Cam had invaded her dreams. She couldn't seem to stop thinking about him, even when she didn't see him. She'd arranged for him to see Sofie again—but always when the baby was home with Yaya or Andie and Rachel was at work. She needed time to shore up her defenses. To get control of the situation.

But she didn't feel in control now. She reached for the doorbell, bouncing Sofie slightly in her arms. "You ready for this, baby girl?"

The last word was barely out of her mouth when the door whisked open. Cam stood in the entry, his smile broad. "You made it."

"I said I would." *Too defensive. Get it together, Rachel.* She forced a smile. "Is your family all here already?"

His grin widened, as he stepped back, holding the door wide so she could come in. "They were all early. They're pretty excited to meet you."

You must mean Sofie, since she was pretty sure the woman who'd kept the baby a secret from them probably wasn't on their list of favorite people. But Rachel didn't let her fake smile falter. "Great."

"Hi, Sofie!" Cam reached for the baby, his face

radiant as the two of them grinned at each other. "How's my sweet girl?"

Rachel told herself it was logical that she hand Sofie over—she had to take her coat off, after all—but her arms felt empty without the familiar weight and she had to stop herself from snatching her daughter back as soon as she hung her coat on the overflowing coatrack.

"Come on," Cam urged, and Rachel trailed him into a great room with a vaulted ceiling that could easily fit her entire apartment. Three women about Cam's age and an older couple sat on the overstuffed couches clustered around a giant Christmas tree, all of them standing with welcoming smiles as soon as Cam appeared.

"There she is!" the older woman—who could only be Cam's mother—exclaimed. And then they were all clustering around for introductions and a closer look. Rachel stayed where she was, two feet behind Cam and a little to his left, with her smile cemented in place as his parents and sisters gushed over the newest member of their family.

"Look at those cheeks!"

"So precious. Hi there, Sofie. I'm your Auntie Shelby. Your *best* auntie."

"She looks just like you, Cam!"

"Nah, she's way cuter than Cam ever was. Remember the ears?"

Rachel watched Sofie, her chest tight with worry that the baby would be overwhelmed, ready to whisk her back into her arms and give her some distance—but her daughter was studying her new family members calmly from the crook of Cam's arm and seemed perfectly comfortable with the situation. It was Rachel who was quietly losing her mind.

"You must be Rachel." A voice spoke at her elbow and Rachel jumped, glancing down at the shortest woman in the group. "I'm Carly. The oldest and wisest of Cam's sisters. You want a drink?"

"I..." Frankly, she would have loved something to take the edge off, but she didn't want Cam's family to think she immediately reached for alcohol in every stressful situation. And she needed to keep her head. "I'm fine, thanks."

Cam handed Sofie to his mother, who immediately began cooing at the baby, and Carly linked her arm with Rachel's. "Come on. You won't be able to pry that baby out of her arms for a while and I want to meet the woman who was able to put up with my obnoxious little brother long enough to wind up with his kid. We'll have some cider—which I highly recommend with the cinnamon whiskey, but it's your call."

"Carly." Cam's voice held a note of warning.

His sister rolled her eyes. "Relax. I'm not going to tell her *all* of your embarrassing stories."

Rachel couldn't seem to read the mood of the room. Carly was acting like Rachel was Cam's current girlfriend—not the woman who'd broken up with him and had his kid in secret. She was playful and grinning. What had he told his family about her?

"You don't have to do anything she says," Cam said to Rachel. "She isn't the boss of the world, even if she thinks she is."

Cam's parents resumed their places on the couch, his mother balancing Sofie on her knee and pointing toward the Christmas presents. "It's okay," Rachel murmured, letting Carly tug her toward the bar at the other end of the room. The idea of talking to Cam's mother was much scarier than being grilled by his sister.

Or all of his sisters, as it turned out.

The other two joined them at the bar stools, introducing themselves while Carly was pouring cider. Cam went to the couch to sit with his parents and if Rachel strained her ears she could just barely hear their conversation—which seemed to revolve around how much Sofie looked like Cam. Which she did. Rachel had seen the similarities since the day she was born. Her smile. The shape of her eyes.

"So we're all dying to know—" Carly paused the bottle of cinnamon whiskey over one of the glasses, arching her brows. Rachel gave a slight nod and she smiled, splashing whiskey into each of the four cups. "What did he do?"

"Sorry?" Rachel accepted the cup Carly slid her way.

"Cam. What did he do to mess things up with you? We know what he thinks happened, but I want to hear your version."

Rachel glanced at the three women. Carly was clearly trying to make her think she was on Rachel's side, but she sincerely doubted Cam's sisters were nearly as kindly disposed toward her as Carly seemed to want her to believe. Shelby, in particular, didn't have much of a poker face and was constantly fighting a glower.

"He didn't tell me he was married," she said, trying to keep it as simple as possible. "When I found out, I broke up with him. Via text." Might as well get it out there, since he'd probably already told them.

Carly nodded. "When was this?"

"Two years ago September. Right before he moved to LA."

Something sparked in Carly's eyes and her grin turned devilish. "You're Miss September."

That didn't sound good. Rachel's stomach clenched

with the now-familiar fear that she didn't know Cam at all. "Does he have a new girl every month?"

"No." Carly laughed. "God, no. I just remembered—" She turned to her sisters. "Do you remember that? Right before he signed the free agent deal, how he was all stupid happy and evasive for like a month? I *knew* there was a girl."

"No, you didn't," Ashley argued. "You kept telling me he was just having a good season and it was all about the playoff push and the free agency crap making him giddy. *I* was the one who came up with Miss September."

Carly waved away her protest. "Does it really matter which one of us came up with it?"

"It does when it's not you," Ashley insisted.

"Whatever. I'm just excited to meet Miss September."

"I still remember October," Shelby said darkly and the other two sobered.

"Yeah," Carly murmured, and the nervous pit returned to Rachel's stomach. "October was rough."

Rachel didn't know what to say to that. She'd been too mad at Cam to care how he took the break-up—though at the time she'd never seriously considered that he might have taken it hard. Her own October had been pretty lousy. She'd had morning sickness that felt like the plague and she'd been kicking herself repeatedly for doing exactly what her mother had done after a lifetime of trying to be anyone but Andie—all while trying to figure out how the hell her life was going to work with a child.

"Are you originally from Boulder?" Ashley asked, changing the subject when the silence got too tense.

"I am."

"And your parents? They're still here?"

"Sofie and I live with my mom and my grandmother. My father died when I was little, but he was never in the picture." She almost didn't tell them the rest, but it wasn't like they were never going to find out. Might as well get it all out there. The whole sordid drama of her origins. "He was Aaron Cross. The football player?" Recognition lit in Carly's eyes, though the other two didn't seem to know the name. Rachel shrugged, explaining, "He never wore a wedding ring either and there wasn't exactly Google at the time—" Not like now. Rachel really should have Googled Cam's marital status. "So my mom didn't know he was already married with a son until she was five months pregnant with me."

Cam's sisters' eyes all widened in unison. It was Carly who spoke. "Shit. No wonder you wanted to castrate Cam when you found out about Erika."

Rachel flushed. "I don't know about castrate. But it was probably good for him that I didn't have a voodoo doll at the time."

Carly laughed, raising her glass in a toast. "My brother doesn't know how lucky he is."

"And when you found out you were pregnant?" Shelby demanded—apparently having exhausted her resources of playing nice.

"Shelby..." Carly glared at her sister—as if she'd broken some unspoken rule.

"No, she's right. I should have told him." Rachel had the feeling all three of Cam's sisters were protective of him, but Shelby was the most aggressive about it, if the way she held Rachel's gaze was anything to go by. In a way it was almost a relief to have one of them challenge her, stripping away the illusion that they were all chummy.

The anxious knot in her stomach pulsed. "I wish I

had a better explanation. I just freaked out. He was already in LA and I'd convinced myself he was the kind of guy the baby and I would be better off without. It's no excuse, but I wasn't really thinking clearly and all I can do is try to do better now. I am trying to do better." Even if it wasn't always easy, letting him back into her life.

Shelby's face stayed impassive, like in her mind the jury was still out on that, but Carly reached over and gently clinked her glass against Rachel's. "That's all any of us can do. To the future."

Ashley raised her glass, grinning. "To the future." And even Shelby reluctantly tapped her glass to her sister's.

Maybe, just maybe, the future would be something worth toasting.

*****

"Aren't you just the smartest baby? Yes, you are."

Cam tried to focus on his mother cooing at Sofie, but his attention kept drifting to where Rachel was being interrogated by his sisters. He wished he could hear what they were talking about. Rachel looked as prickly as she had since she walked in the door—but at least she didn't look any *more* prickly, so maybe he should take that as a good sign.

She'd been avoiding him. They were both trying to adjust to the situation, but he felt like they were two lions warily circling one another—or a pitcher trying to figure out a batter's strengths without a scouting report. They were both figuring it out as they went along and the awkwardness was digging underneath his skin.

He wanted to be able to talk to her. He wanted her to be able to talk to him. He wanted a moment with her when things didn't feel stilted and uncomfortable. And he wanted to not be jealous of his own sisters because she was actually talking to them.

"Cam?"

He glanced up, catching his mother watching him with a knowing look. He cleared his throat, trying to clear away the indecision. "I should go rescue Rachel."

Thankfully, his mother didn't comment on the fact that Rachel didn't look like she needed rescuing. Carly and Ashley were laughing and even Shelby seemed to have lost some of the sharp distrust she'd carried around since they found out about Sofie. Rachel's smile was more hesitant, but it was peeking out around the edges—and he was jealous again. Jealous that someone else had made her smile.

God, he was an idiot.

"Are you three playing nice?" he asked as he approached—and watched Rachel's spine stiffen. She glanced over to where his mother was showing Sofie an alphabet toy. "She's fine," he assured her. "And my mother's in heaven. Thank you for this."

"Of course," she murmured, as his sisters stood up and began moving toward the baby.

"Time to go dote on my niece," Carly declared, leaving Cam and Rachel alone at the bar.

Rachel watched the exodus, not meeting his eyes.

"You okay?" he asked softly. She was so contained, like she was holding herself together.

Her gaze flicked over to his then back to the tableau in front of the tree. "I'm good. I just…it's a lot."

"You're telling me. A week ago I was going to a meeting about a bachelor auction and now everything is different."

"Not everything. You better still be at that auction. I don't have time to find another headlining Bachelor. I already have half a dozen emails I need to reply to about the fundraiser to make sure everything is in place. I haven't had time to do my Christmas shopping—which is usually done and wrapped under the tree by now—and now there's meetings with you and your family to fit into a schedule that was already too full."

"I could help," he offered. "I could take Sofie while you do your shopping..." He trailed off, seeing the refusal on her face before she said a word.

"No, it's fine. I'll manage. I always do. It just feels like something has to give and I don't want it to be Sofie's Christmas. My mother was always scrambling until the last minute too, wrapping my presents on Christmas Eve to try to get them in before the wire. I want Sofie to have the chance to anticipate, to let the excitement of the season build."

Cam arched a brow. "She really won't know the difference."

"But I will."

"Don't you think you're stressing yourself out over nothing? At this age, she's going to play with the box. If anything, she's going to pick up on the fact that her mom is putting unnecessary stress on herself trying to make everything perfect." It was the Christmas tree all over again. "Besides, if you force everything around Sofie to be perfect all the time, what do you think she's going to think she has to be?"

He only meant that she needed to try to enjoy the things that weren't part of her plans, to laugh at the things she couldn't control. He knew firsthand how hard it was to keep up the appearance of perfection—but he saw his mistake the second Rachel raised her eyes to his.

CHAPTER TWELVE

Anger rushed through Rachel like a flash flood. "Are you implying that I'm giving Sofie a perfectionism complex?"

How dare he? How dare he criticize her parenting? She was doing her best, damn it. She didn't want Sofie to be perfect. She wanted everything to be perfect *for* Sofie. There was a difference. A huge one. She would rearrange her entire life for her child—had already done so in a hundred ways—and here he was in his first week as a father thinking he could tell her all the ways she was messing up their daughter?

Cam held up his hands in surrender. "Okay, that isn't what I meant—"

"What did you mean then? Explain to me how I misunderstood."

"I just meant maybe don't sweat the small stuff."

"The small stuff, as you put it, is what she's going to remember. They're the patterns that are going to shape her entire life. She's learning right now. She's absorbing everything—so everything matters."

"Which is a good way to give yourself a nervous breakdown. Some things are outside of our control and she's gotta learn to take the unexpected and roll with it. To keep playing even after an error or a strikeout. To just play at all without worrying about the future."

"Says the player," she snapped.

"Yeah. A *ball player*. Not a *player* player. I never played you, Rachel. And I'm not going to apologize for wanting you to relax and have a little fun."

"My life is fun!" She knew how to have fun, damn it. "Sofie's life is fun. We play all the time."

And if it was all scheduled playtime that was just the way life had to be. She needed the order. She needed the plan. She'd tried spontaneity when she first met Cam and look what had happened. She couldn't let her guard down and be impulsive. The universe was waiting to smack you in the face when you did.

"We should go." The words were stiff, the muscles in her neck tight with tension. "It's getting late and I don't want to upset Sofie's sleep schedule."

"Rachel…don't leave angry."

"I'm not." This feeling, this wasn't anger. It was frustration. Exhaustion. The need to go home and wrap herself in a protective cocoon, because she felt like she literally could not take one more thing without completely falling apart. "But we do need to go."

The goodbyes took a while.

Cam took charge and shouldered his family's disappointment by being the one to announce that Sofie and Rachel had to leave. He stood firm against the wave of protests so she didn't have to, but it still took several minutes for everyone to hug Sofie. Carly and Ashley hugged Rachel and she tried not to stiffen in their arms as the entire group migrated toward the door. Carly handed her a card and urged her to call anytime. Cam's mother patted her arm and told her they should make sure they had a chance to talk next time—and Rachel smiled and nodded, though thinking about next time made her stomach roil.

They were so nice. Behaving so perfectly. The freaking dream in-laws. And she felt like she was braced against it, waiting for the other shoe to drop. Sure, they were nice on the surface, but they had to hate her, didn't they? They must think she'd done Cam wrong. They must be mad at her for keeping Sofie a secret. The smiles just made her feel nervous. And guilty.

She'd never been so relieved to get out of a house.

Cam walked her to her car, carrying Sofie tucked against his chest. He watched Rachel buckle her into her car seat and spoke softly when she tugged the straps to check their snugness.

"Thank you for coming tonight."

Of course she'd come. What kind of person would refuse when he wanted his daughter to meet his parents and siblings? Even if part of her had wanted to slow everything down, she hadn't felt like she had a choice. Ever since Cam had come back into her life, she'd felt boxed in, and it was *exhausting*. The soft gratitude in his voice just made her feel worse. Like an ogre for wanting to snatch Sofie away and run home.

"Of course," she murmured, closing Sofie's car door and opening her own. "Thanks for inviting us."

"I'll see you soon?"

The hopeful lilt in his voice was another subtle, grating push. He just wanted to spend time with his daughter. If she said no, she was automatically cast as the bad guy, but sometimes she simply didn't have the emotional energy to say yes. He didn't want her, he wanted Sofie—he'd made that clear in the last week in the way he only called to try to see the baby—but she was the one who had to make it work. She was the one being backed into a corner over and over.

"Sure," she murmured, keeping it vague, trying to

make her escape. "G'night, Cam."

"Good night." He stepped back as she closed the door and started the engine. He stood there watching, making the hair raise on her neck until she drove away.

Sofie was babbling to herself in the backseat and Rachel concentrated on the sounds. "Did you have fun tonight, baby?"

Sofie babbled cheerfully back, none the worse for having been passed from stranger to stranger for the last hour. She'd always been good with being passed around. So tiny, and already so confident, so independent. Was that Cam's DNA at work? She rarely clung to Rachel, only pitching a fit and insisting on her mama when she was tired or sick. Yaya said it was a sign that she was secure that she was loved and safe, and that she trusted the adults in her life to never give her to someone who wasn't trustworthy—but a perverse part of Rachel sometimes wished Sofie needed her and only her a little bit more.

The babble had quieted by the time they arrived back at the apartment. Sofie slumped in her car seat, fast asleep. Rachel didn't put much faith in her chances of getting Sofie upstairs and into bed without her waking up and being fussy for three hours, but she carried her up the stairs in stealth mode. Sofie stirred once as Rachel shifted her to unlock the door, but she settled back on her shoulder with a sleepy sigh as the door creaked open.

Her mother was sitting on the couch, watching *Love Actually* for the ten thousandth time, and Rachel put a finger to her lips to urge her to silence before she could greet them. She toed off her shoes and crept into the bedroom—

And made it all the way to the crib before Sofie

opened her eyes and began a ninety minute campaign to reject sleep.

The final scenes of *Love Actually* were playing when Rachel finally dragged herself into the kitchen to reward herself for surviving bedtime with a cup of cocoa and to get ready for the next day. Her mother sniffled into a tissue as she watched the ending, crying as if she hadn't memorized the entire film word-for-word.

Andie hit the mute button as the final song began to play. "How'd it go tonight?" she asked as Rachel sank down on the couch beside her with her cocoa.

"They were great. Everything was great," she said, knowing her tone sounded anything but great, but too worn down to infuse false enthusiasm into her voice.

Her mother rested her hand on top of Rachel's on the couch. "I know it's awkward now, but you'll be grateful Sofie has those relationships in the long run. I always wished you'd had more contact with your father's side."

Rachel pulled her hand away, disguising the move by wrapping both hands around her mug as she lifted her cocoa to her lips.

She hadn't had more contact with her father's side because her father didn't want anyone to know she existed. It might have tarnished his perfect image. Big Aaron, the golden god of the NFL, who was practically sainted in his hometown.

And then there was her mother, who always talked about him like he was a hero and not the married man who had lied to her and strung her along. Rachel barely remembered him. He died when she was so young that most of her memories of him came from the stories people told, but he must have been charming because no one ever seemed to hold him accountable for his actions.

"Weren't you mad at him?" she asked, the words

erupting from deep inside where she'd pushed them down a thousand times.

Her mother frowned. "Cameron?"

"My father. He lied to you."

Andie grimaced, her expressive face twisting. "I wasn't *happy* about it, but I suppose I didn't see what holding onto anger toward him would accomplish."

"Accomplish? It would show him he can't do whatever he wants all the time—that there are consequences."

"But I didn't want the consequences," Andie said simply. "I didn't want to shut him out of our lives. I had to decide if I was going to be okay with what had happened in the past so we could have a future."

Rachel set her cocoa down too hard on the end table. "But you didn't have a future. He was never going to leave his wife."

"I know. And I knew then. I wasn't a complete fool. There were only so many times I could talk myself into ignoring the way he danced around the truth. Always evading the question. I'd ask him if he still loved her and he'd never just deny it—he'd tell me I was silly. But he didn't lie."

Rachel remembered those arguments—though she'd been so young at the time she wasn't sure whether she remembered the actual arguments with her father or the later fights between Andie and Yaya about him. *Don't be ridiculous, Andie. I love you.* As if that was a get out of jail free card.

She'd always thought her mother was gullible, but if she hadn't believed his crap…

"But *why*? Why stay with him when you knew?"

She shrugged. "He was your father."

Rachel leaned back as if she could physically avoid

the implication of those words. "Please tell me you didn't continue an affair with a married man for me."

Her mother made a small frustrated noise. "He wasn't just a married man. You always try to oversimplify things. To make them black and white, right and wrong, when the truth is usually somewhere in the middle. You've always wanted me to regret getting involved with him, to blame him for lying or be mad at myself for trusting him—but I'm not sorry. I'm *glad* I did what I did. He wasn't perfect, but I truly loved your father—but more than that, I love *you*. You're the best thing that ever happened to me and I'm never going to be sorry for the way you came into my life. Not ever. I thought you would understand that when you had Sofie."

Rachel looked away, unprepared for her mother's passionate words.

"I never set out to be the other woman," she went on. "It's not like I wanted that for myself. Sometimes life just happens. It can't always be planned. It can't always be perfect. But that's the best part. The things we don't expect can be the biggest blessings. And yes, I felt like a fool, and yes, I was mad at him, but what good would it do anyone to hold onto those feelings? I had you. I wanted you to know your father. And our family may not have been normal or *right*, by some people's definitions, but I was going to make the best of it. For us. Holding onto anger will eat you alive."

Rachel studied her mother in the light of the Christmas tree and the reflected glow of the muted television that was now playing a rerun of *The Big Bang Theory*.

Her mother was always late, always behind on the rent. It had been easy to dismiss her as a beacon of bad judgment. Irresponsible Andie. She'd been calling her mother that in her mind so long it was hard to remember when it had started. Middle school? Earlier? Rachel had become hyper-organized as a defense mechanism, learning to lie to her mom about when she needed to be places so she would actually get there when she wanted to. She'd always seen herself as a tower of responsibility—which was why it had stung so much when she found herself following in her mother's pregnant-by-a-married-man footsteps.

She'd seen her mother's past as a litany of mistakes, not of choices. She hadn't noticed Andie making the best of a bad situation. Too focused on what should have happened. Too angry that Andie wasn't angry.

"I'm sorry, Mama."

"What? Oh, honey, you never have to apologize to me."

Rachel shook her head, shame climbing up her throat. "Yes, I do. You're a great mom."

Andie laughed. "I don't know about that. But I do my best. And there's nothing I wouldn't do for you. You know that."

She did. She'd always known.

Maybe she was too rigid. Trying to force things toward perfection a little too much. Maybe Cam was just a little bit right and she needed to be more like her mother.

Her mother always made the best of things—even their crazy, dramatic Christmases. Her mother always waited until the absolute last minute to do things and rushed through them in a frenzy, but it was because she was trying to do too much, not because she didn't care.

Not that she wanted to be as disorganized as her mother, but Andie was amazing at letting past mistakes and frustrations roll off her back. Just like Cam. It had always annoyed Rachel—the way she never seemed to learn from her mistakes because they genuinely didn't bother her—but maybe she needed to take a page out of her mother's book and learn not to hold onto things quite so much. Her mother didn't apologize for all the ways her chaos impacted the lives around her, but she also never needed an apology. She could look past her hurt and focus on the good, and the future.

Rachel scooted closer to her mother on the couch, resting her head on her mom's shoulder. "There's nothing I wouldn't do for you too, Mama."

Her mother put her arm around her. "I know, baby. I've always known."

And just like that, all was forgiven. The power of a mother's love.

If only everything could be so easy with Cam.

CHAPTER THIRTEEN

"Hold up, dumbass."

Cam didn't miss a step as he walked to his car, speaking over his shoulder to his oldest and most annoying sister. "You can't actually expect me to respond to that."

"And yet you do." Carly jogged to catch up to him. "And I'll stop calling you that when you wise up and stop screwing up your life."

Since she wasn't going away, like a fly buzzing around his head, he turned to face her, leaning against his Land Rover. "I assume you're going to tell me how I'm screwing up my life?"

"What are sisters for?"

"Unconditional love and support?"

"I think that's grandparents. Sisters are supposed to keep you humble and tell you when you're screwing up."

He cocked his head. "I don't think that's actually a rule."

"Well, it's my rule." Carly paused to wave as their parents drove past them in the Cayenne he'd bought for them last Christmas, followed by Ashley and her brood. Shelby had already headed home. When they were alone in the driveway, Carly turned to him, hands on hips. "What do you want to happen with Rachel?"

He'd had a feeling that was where this was going. He should have gotten in the car and driven away. "What do you mean?"

"Am I supposed to pretend I didn't notice how protective you were of her all night?"

He folded his arms. "She was uncomfortable. It's overwhelming, meeting all of you."

"So that's why you couldn't take your eyes off her?" Carly asked skeptically. "Because she was overwhelmed and you're such a good guy?"

"Is there a point to all this?" Cam gave his sister his most intimidating frown, the glower that put rookie pitchers in line when they were too full of themselves to let him call the freaking game. His sister merely smiled.

"Do you have a plan to win her back?"

"I thought you were rooting for the librarian."

"That was before I found out Rachel was Miss September."

Cam frowned. "Am I supposed to know what that means?"

"Two years ago you were like a robot. You never admitted you were upset by your divorce, never showed any emotion—which was frankly a little creepy—but I figured you were just putting on a good face. You've never been good at talking about mushy feelings stuff, and it had to suck to be pissed at her but feel like you couldn't really be mad at her because she might be dying—"

"I wasn't mad at her. You were the one who hated her."

"Well, yeah, you're my kid brother. She was the enemy on principle—but it was hard to hate her when she was sick and she'd always been so nice to everyone. It was you I worried about. Robot Cam. But then all of a sudden something changed. It was September and you were optimistic and dopily happy. We'd never seen you like that and Miss September was what we called the mystery girl we all figured you were dating."

Cam tipped his face back toward the house so she couldn't see his eyes. He hadn't realized he'd been so obvious.

"And now tonight, the way you were with her—it was like you were aware of where she was at every second. You were never like that with Erika. You guys were friends and you worked as a couple because you cared about one another, but you were never protective of her. She was never *yours*."

Cam worked his jaw, still studying the Christmas lights on the house so he didn't have to meet his sister's eyes. "Rachel doesn't want anything to do with me like that."

"Can you blame her?"

His gaze snapped to hers at that. "I thought you were on my side."

"I'm on the side of love, baby brother, but I talked to her tonight and I gotta say, I can see her side of it. I don't know if I would have done any differently."

"Are you kidding? She hid Sofie from me."

"Why didn't you tell her about Erika? Why let her find out like that?"

He'd asked himself that a thousand times. He'd had so many reasons at the time, all of which felt inadequate now. "I was waiting for the right moment." At her look, he rolled his eyes. "We were having fun and everything was easy and light. That time with Rachel was my escape and I didn't want to bring all the real shit going on with Erika into it."

"Did you know about her background? Her parents.

Her baggage with married men."

"I knew," he admitted.

Carly rolled her eyes. "A not-quite-ex-wife you were supporting through cancer even though she'd dumped your ass when she got diagnosed might have been something you needed to mention."

"I wasn't trying to hide it from her. It's not like I never would have told her. I was just putting it off. We'd only been together a few weeks. I thought there'd be time."

"Really?"

He met Carly's steady gaze, admitting the truth. "I was afraid she'd run. I wanted her to fall for me before I told her. I wanted her to be invested, so she'd stay." And he'd never liked talking about the hard stuff.

He didn't share his troubles, not with anyone. *Pay no attention to the man behind the curtain. Never let them see the effort.* It was all about making it look easy. He didn't want to admit his own lack of perfection.

And here he'd been giving Rachel a hard time about her own perfectionism complex. God, what a mess.

Carly sighed. "You still suck at communication, you know that? If you don't tell her who you really are and what's really going on with you, it isn't you she's falling for. It's just the perfect image you're projecting. You gotta be honest. About what you want. About why you're scared you won't get it. Talk to her."

"I've been talking to her." He wasn't making the same mistakes.

"Yeah? So she knows why Erika left? And you've told her that you still have feelings for her?"

"I do not still have feelings for Erika," he protested.

"For *Rachel,* dumbass. You've told *Rachel* that birds sing when she walks into a room and you want to be more than just her baby daddy? But that you've had a whole *no one will ever love me* complex ever since Erika left?

"I don't have a complex. You're horrible, you know that?"

"I love you," Carly reminded him. "And I want you to be happy."

"Not everyone is happiest when they're talking everything to death. She could completely shut me down."

"True," she acknowledged. "But it doesn't hurt to try."

"You're not the one laying your heart open."

"Also true." She folded her arms, staring up at him. "So I guess you have to decide if you'd rather lay your heart open or pine with unrequited love for your baby mama for the rest of your life. Tough call."

"You're the worst." He reached for her, tugging her into his arms.

"Love you too. Dumbass. Now go get your girl."

*****

The text was making her nervous. *Can we talk?* sounded entirely too ominous.

Rachel had just finished picking up the wine donated for the mystery bags at the Russell House fundraiser when the message came in on the morning after Sofie met Cam's family.

She'd promised herself she was going to stop assuming the worst and try to be more flexible—but that was easier said than done as she pulled into the TD Events parking lot. Picking up the wine hadn't taken as long as she'd scheduled for it, so she'd told Cam she had a window of time if he wanted to meet at the TD Events offices right away.

He'd texted back almost instantly that he was on his way.

Reminding herself to stop worrying, she began unloading the wine. It would need to be brought to the hotel ballroom on the day of the event, but in the meantime her office was the only place she could think of to store a hundred bottles of wine where they wouldn't freeze. She was loading the fourth box onto the hand trolley when Cam's Land Rover pulled into the spot next to hers—and she reminded herself again not to give in to the panic bunnies.

She was turning over a new leaf. She wasn't trying to control things so much. She would be good with spontaneity and surprises. She *would*.

"Hey. Need a hand?"

It was ingrained to say no, to insist that she could do it herself, but she was determined to stop shooting herself in the foot. "Sure. That'd be great. Thanks."

He wore jeans and a sweater, but still managed to look like a GQ cover spread as he hitched up a box and stacked it on top of the others on the hand trolley. He tilted it to maneuver it toward the building and Rachel shut the tailgate before rushing ahead to hold the door open.

In the lobby, Cam tilted his head to read the label on the boxes as they waited for the world's slowest elevator. "Big party?"

"It's for the fundraiser. We're having mystery bags—wine, whiskey, chocolates, coffee—pretty much anything we could get people to donate. Some bags will be more valuable than others, but for twenty-five bucks the patrons can roll the dice and choose a mystery bag. It's another way to engage the people who want to support the hospital but can't afford to bid on the big ticket items." She nodded toward him and Cam flushed.

"It feels a little weird to *be* a big ticket item. I hope people actually bid. It's just batting practice."

"People will bid," she assured him as the elevator arrived. She stepped in first, holding the door open as he wheeled in the trolley. "Trust me."

"I am." The doors closed as she tried not to shiver at the throaty promise behind the words. "You're good at this. I don't think I ever really thought about all the details that go into an event like this."

"Trista had most of it set up before she went on vacation." The elevator door opened on the third floor and Rachel held the door again as he maneuvered the wine out. "Though the mystery bags were one of my suggestions. I'd seen a similar thing done at another event and recommended it when we were doing our initial planning."

She led the way down the hall toward her office, trying not to flush self-consciously when her colleagues glanced up to watch her pass with Cameron Cole.

They unloaded the wine, stacking it in the corner of her office, and went back down for the next load. The conversation remained light and easy, general chit-chat about Cam's charity involvement and the various events that Rachel had coordinated in the past. She could almost convince herself that she'd been worrying over nothing—except she was reasonably certain he hadn't come to chat about the fundraiser.

Cam waited until they'd piled the last box of wine into her office. The tower of alcohol made the already cramped confines of her office feel even more claustrophobic. He nodded toward the open doorway. "Do you mind if I close the door?"

Rachel forced a smile that she hoped didn't look as

sickly as it felt. "Go ahead." She moved around behind her desk, waving him toward the chair opposite and hoping the businesslike approach would set the tone. "What can I do for you?"

He lowered himself into the chair. "I was hoping we could talk about—well, about a lot of things I guess. I'm sorry to bother you at work—"

"No, this is a good time." She folded her hands on the desk, keeping her expression polite. "What's on your mind?"

"My sisters like you."

She blinked, startled by the apparent non sequitur. "Um, I liked them too."

"Carly called me an idiot for not telling you about Erika before—and she was right."

"Cam. You've already apologized—"

"I know, but I didn't explain."

"You said she had cancer," she argued, not sure she wanted more of an explanation. It felt entirely too personal.

"Ovarian cancer. Pretty advanced by the time they found it. She'd been ignoring her symptoms, putting off going to the doctor because I'd started talking about having kids and it was easier for her to avoid going to her gynecologist than it was to tell me she didn't want to go off birth control after all. We'd talked about it when we first got together and she didn't want kids at the time, but we were twenty-two then and I figured she'd change her mind. When I started talking about being ready, she didn't object, so I assumed she was onboard. The diagnosis—she called it a wake-up call. She said life was too short and we wanted different things and she couldn't pretend anymore. We'd been going through the motions for a while. Doing all the things you should do without ever really talking or connecting."

"Cam..." She shifted in her chair, uncomfortable with how much he was revealing.

"At first, I thought she'd snap out of it. I thought it was a reaction to the diagnosis—and it was, but she never changed her mind. She moved out that week, went to live with her sister. I talked her into putting off filing for divorce—she had access to the best doctors in Colorado as long as she stayed on my insurance. She kept doing work with the team's charities. She worried that the press would come after me, twist it to look like I'd left her when she was sick, so she always denied the separation rumors. She told people she was living with her sister because I had to travel with the team so it was easier to manage her treatment living with someone who wasn't always coming and going. By the time I met you, she was in remission, but we hadn't filed for divorce because the doctors said there was still a chance of recurrence."

Rachel swallowed. "Why didn't you say anything?"

"I should have. I just—when I met you, it was like *my* wake up call. I'd been going through the motions, feeling like I was faking everything, and you felt real. I never had to pretend with you. It just felt right and I didn't want to bring all that baggage into it." He shook his head. "You came into my life at a really complicated moment and I didn't handle it well. And then when you left it was like the rug being yanked out from under me. I should have told you—I don't want to have any secrets from you. I want you to feel like you can talk to me, not just about Sofie. I want..." He trailed off and when he spoke again she had the feeling he'd changed what he was going to say. "I want us to trust each other."

Her chest felt tight as she swallowed thickly. "I want

that too," she murmured, though she wasn't sure how good she was going to be at it. They had so much history between them now. Could they come back from that? Could they trust one another again?

She bit her lip. "So how do we do that?"

CHAPTER FOURTEEN

It wasn't a date.

Rachel kept telling herself that. She and Cam were meeting to go Christmas shopping for Sofie together while her mother watched the baby. That was all it was. An effort at co-parenting and being more open and trusting with one another.

But she was as nervous as if it was a date.

Ever since the conversation in her office when he'd told her about his ex, she'd been finding it harder and harder to keep him at a safe mental distance. She found herself remembering the first time they met, the memories no longer twisted by bitterness and recriminations.

She'd been volunteering at a cystic fibrosis fundraiser TD Events was throwing, all part of her plan to meet Trista and score an interview with the premiere event planner in the Denver area. She hadn't noticed Cam, totally focused on making a good impression on Trista—and it had worked. At the end of the event, Trista had asked her to come by for an interview in a couple weeks and Rachel had let herself celebrate with a single glass of champagne on the balcony.

She hadn't expected Cam to join her with a fresh bottle and a glass of his own. She was usually so guarded around men, so careful with her heart, but he'd congratulated her—somehow knowing she was celebrating without even knowing why—and something had clicked into place. She didn't remember the details, didn't remember what they'd talked about. She only remembered the feeling. Like she was alive for the first time, just like he'd said, electrified from the inside by a spark she'd never known was missing.

She wasn't impulsive, but with him she had been. And it had been magical. But could they really get that magic back? Did she want to?

Cam rang the doorbell promptly at six. Rachel had barely had time to rush home and change after work—which meant she hadn't had time to obsess over what she was wearing. Much. She was barefoot in jeans and a soft red sweater when she rushed to the door, past her mother spooning yogurt into Sofie's mouth at the table.

Cam stood on the front step—and once again he looked like something out of a freaking magazine. Coat open, hands shoved into the front pockets of faded jeans, the beginning of beard scruff on his cheeks. Then he smiled and her chest tightened at the familiar grin. "Hey."

"Hey." Heat warmed her cheeks and she told herself it was just a reaction to the cold outside. "Come on in. I just need to grab my shoes and my purse."

He came into the entryway as Rachel rushed to find shoes and socks—and his grin turned outright dopey as he clapped eyes on Sofie. "Hey there, baby girl! Whatcha got there? Is that yogurt?"

Rachel ducked into the bedroom, giving herself a quick and ruthless lecture on keeping her head. Just because he was insanely hot and went gooey at the sight of their daughter and actually appeared to be a genuinely good human being who would financially support his ex-wife through cancer even after she left him...she'd lost her train of thought. She'd been going in a don't-fall-for-him direction, but she couldn't seem to remember the reasons why.

Cam was making faces at Sofie when she came out of the bedroom, and Andie was trying to hide a smile—and failing—as the baby giggled.

"Ready to go?" Rachel asked, all business. One of the ornaments on the tree looked like it had fallen down to a lower branch, but she forced herself not to fix it with Cam watching, moving instead toward the door and putting on her coat.

Cam clapped his hands. "Let's do this."

Rachel looked past him to her mother. "We won't be long."

"Take your time. We're good," she assured them, smiling in a way that was entirely too hopeful.

This isn't a date.

Even if he did put his hand on her arm as they crossed the parking lot toward his car. It was icy. He was being courteous.

But the touch still made her shiver and words rushed out of her mouth to cover her nerves. "I already ordered most of Sofie's presents from my mom and Yaya and me. I'm not sure what you had in mind to get for her, but I can point you toward things that she isn't already getting—"

"Didn't I just hear you bemoaning the fact that you hadn't had time to do your Christmas shopping?" Cam hit the key fob to unlock his Range Rover and opened her door for her—which was *not* a date thing to do. He probably did that for everyone.

"That was two days ago," she reminded him.

"Of course it was. My bad." He laughed as he shut

her door and rounded the hood to climb into the driver's seat.

She shoved more words into the car with them. "There was one thing I couldn't get for as good a deal online—this interactive Sesame Street learning toy with really good reviews—so I put it on hold at Target, though they didn't have it in stock at the close one, so I'll need to head up to the Longmont store, but I can do that on my own if that doesn't fit into the schedule tonight. What did you have in mind?"

He arched a brow as he clicked his seatbelt. "I have to have a plan?"

"It's easier to figure out where we should be going if we know what you're looking for."

Cam shrugged, turning on the engine of the posh SUV. "I figured something would grab me."

"Right." She forcibly restrained herself from pulling out the list of possible present options she'd made on her phone. This was Cam's idea. Cam's present for Sofie.

He glanced over at her as he pulled out of the parking space. "It's going to drive you crazy, isn't it? Not having a plan."

She pressed her lips together, but the words burst out. "It just sounds like a really inefficient way of going about it. Where were you even going to go?"

"A mall? Or better yet, we'll go pick up your Sesame Street thing and see if anything jumps out at us up there. Does that plan meet your standards?"

"I like being organized," she defended against the teasing note in his voice. "There's nothing wrong with being a planner."

"You're absolutely right," he agreed. She studied him for traces of sarcasm, but he seemed sincere. "As long as you don't miss the spontaneous stuff."

"Spontaneous Christmas shopping sounds like a good way of ending up with things that don't suit anyone on your list."

"True. But if you only look for the things that are on your carefully planned list, you might miss out on things that people would love even more. You've gotta be open to the unexpected."

"I'm open. I'm not incapable of seeing things that aren't part of my plans," she argued as he pointed the car toward Longmont. "I just like knowing what I'm looking for and where I can find it. It's efficient."

"And I love it." He grinned. "How is the world's most symmetrical tree, by the way?"

She rolled her eyes, trying not to remember that one ornament and how it had slipped down two branches. "Were you this annoying when we met before?"

"Absolutely. It's my charm. You were helpless in the face of it."

"Was I though?"

"Definitely." His grin was broad—and unsettlingly intimate—when he flicked a glance at her. Thankfully he was driving and couldn't hold her gaze because she probably would have turned to putty if he had. Where had her defenses against him gone?

"So Sofie's into Sesame Street, huh?" At the comment, Rachel glanced over, frowning, and Cam explained, "The toy?"

"Right, yeah, it's, um, educational. And she's a little obsessed with Elmo."

"Good to know." He stared out the front window, giving her a chance to admire his profile. "Thanks for doing this, by the way. I wouldn't have the first clue what to get her. It's weird. Not knowing what she likes. Though I'm going to. By her birthday, I'm gonna have this down."

It was the first mention of the future and Rachel tried not to react to it. Sofie's birthday was in the middle of the baseball season. He'd be back in LA, doing his job. How often would they even see him? Or would he expect her to bring Sofie to LA? Would he fly them out on weekends? Put them up in fancy hotels…or with him? It felt too soon to even be thinking about things like that when she didn't even know what the next two weeks would bring, but she couldn't seem to stop her brain once it burrowed down that rabbit hole.

He asked what other things Sofie liked and Rachel kept up a running monologue of Sofie stories during the thirty minute drive up to Longmont.

The Christmas crowds were out in force, even on a weeknight, and the parking lot was packed when they arrived. Cam pulled into the first available space and Rachel's story about Sofie's bizarre *I will eat only broccoli* phase trailed off as they exited the car.

"I'll go straight to the pick-up counter and meet you back in the toy section when I'm done." She moved quickly toward the store, focusing on her purpose and not the man at her side—until they stepped through the automatic doors.

Cam caught her arm, guiding her out of the way of a woman who wasn't watching where she was pushing her cart, and every cell in Rachel's body hummed with awareness of him. He released her almost immediately, but she'd lost her train of thought, her brain scrambling to reboot after the incidental touch. How was she supposed to get through this night if he couldn't even brush her arm without her hormones going crazy?

And she apparently wasn't the only one who was hyper aware of him. Even in the hurried rush of pre-

Christmas shopping days, Rachel saw several harried mommies give him a lingering glance, their steps hitching as they walked past. Did they recognize him? Or was it just his unfair GQ good looks?

It was tempting to stare them down, marking him clearly as *hers,* but he wasn't. Not like that. So she forced herself to turn toward the pick-up counter. "I'll see you back there."

Cam looked lost for a moment, but he rallied quickly, saluting and starting toward the back of the store as Rachel headed toward the—thankfully short—pick-up line.

Fifteen minutes later she had the Sesame Street toy paid for and tucked into a reusable shopping bag as she headed back toward the kid-topia at the back of the store.

She half expected to find Cam surrounded by a swarm of helpful mommies batting their eyelashes at him—but what she saw when she stepped into the first toy aisle might actually have been more horrifying.

"No."

Cam stood with one hand on a shopping cart that was literally overflowing with a lion stuffed animal that looked to be life-sized. It had a giant red bow around its neck and Rachel started shaking her head as she approached.

"Sofie does not need a stuffed animal the size of a small horse."

"No one *needs* a stuffed animal," Cam conceded, but his eyes were gleaming with excitement. "But don't you think she'd love it?"

She would. But it was wildly impractical. "We don't have the space. Can you imagine that in my apartment? It's bigger than most of the furniture."

"So we keep it at my place," Cam offered instantly.

Rachel shot him a look, but he missed it as he patted the stuffed lion on the head, already off and running with his new plan. "I should set up a space for her over there anyway. Get some toys. A crib so she can stay overnight—"

Rachel's stomach knotted at the thought of Sofie spending a night away from her. Things were moving too fast again, faster than she could keep up. Then she spotted the price tag. *"Two hundred and eighty dollars?* Are you kidding me?"

"It's a showstopper."

"It's pointless. And ridiculously overpriced."

Cam shrugged. "What's Christmas for?"

That certainly answered the question of whether he was going to try to spoil Sofie with extravagant gifts. Irritation snapped through her. "Am I always going to have to be the rational one while you always get to be the fun one who breaks the rules?"

"I didn't know there was a No Giant Stuffed Animals rule."

She narrowed her eyes at him. "That isn't what I meant and you know it. Is that the kind of parent you want to be? The Fun Dad?"

* * * * *

Cam met her eyes, his enthusiasm retreating at the irritation in hers. Was that really what she thought of him? That he only wanted to be the Fun Dad? That he would balk at the first hint of responsibility?

His fingers sank into the silky-soft fur of the plush lion. He'd just wanted to get it right.

"I don't know what kind of dad I'm going to be," he said slowly, after a long moment. "I'm still figuring it out. I just…I don't know her. And I want her to love the first thing I give her." He'd already missed so much. He looked away from her, back at the lion. "If you really don't want me to get it, I won't get it."

"I'm sorry," Rachel whispered, and he glanced up to see guilt written across her face. "I'm being a jerk. I know you want it to be perfect for her, just like I do. I can't be mad at you for being excited about Christmas with her when I'm the same way." Her gaze flicked past him to the lion. "They have giant stuffed animals at Costco too," she offered. "I don't know if they have a lion, but they definitely have bears and dogs. They're almost as big and I think they're only thirty or forty bucks." She swallowed. "She'd love one."

Cam's heart lifted. "Yeah?"

"Yeah." Rachel's lips quirked in a small, shy smile and he couldn't stop the massive smile that spread across his face.

"See? Teamwork. We've got this."

She laughed softly, but wouldn't meet his eyes, taking a sudden interest in the toys around him as he replaced the massive lion on the shelf.

She was still so hesitant with him, so reluctant to let him in, but he could feel the momentum shifting, like a game where he was behind by five runs and the first few batters started to get on base. He was closer to winning her back with each smile—and he wasn't going to stop trying to earn them.

CHAPTER FIFTEEN

"Rachel Persopoulos, are you dating *Cameron Cole* and you didn't even tell me?"

"What? No!" Rachel nearly streaked a black line across the entire Russell House fundraiser seating chart as her head snapped up and her arm jerked. JoJo stood in the doorway of her office, holding a cream-colored Christmas present with a big red ribbon. "Why would you think that?"

They weren't dating. The other night had most definitely not been a date. They were building trust as co-parents. That's all it was. She needed to remember that. To keep a minimum safe distance.

"This just arrived for you." JoJo sing-songed, coming into her office and lifting the present, curiosity bright in her eyes. "A certain baseball player dropped it off himself."

Rachel flushed, reaching for the package. Neatly wrapped in crisp cream paper with a sparkling red ribbon, it was a rectangular shirt box, lighter than she'd expected as she took it from JoJo's hands. "I'm sure it's nothing," she mumbled, flipping open the card.

Not all gifts have to be practical. I couldn't resist. C.

"Why is Cameron Cole bringing you presents? Please tell me you're secretly knocking boots with one of the hottest bachelors in the greater Denver area."

JoJo was her best friend at work—possibly her best friend period, though neither of them had much time for girls' nights. They'd both been pregnant at the same time—JoJo with twins—and JoJo's dramatic recitals of All The Things No One Ever Tells You About Pregnancy had kept Rachel laughing—and sane—through those months. But she hadn't told her about Cam. She hadn't told *anyone* outside of her family about Cam. Though it wasn't a secret anymore.

"It isn't like that." She smoothed the ribbon, her fingertips coming away covered in glitter. "He's Sofie's father."

"Whoa." JoJo's eyes went wide. "Cameron Cole is Dickface the Wonder Douche?"

A choked noise caught in her throat—she'd forgotten JoJo's oh-so-delicate nickname for her ex.

"Why didn't you ever say who he was?" JoJo demanded. Her expressive face contorted as if she couldn't decide on an emotion. "I don't think I can like him anymore. I mean he's hot and always super nice to me, but knowing he left you and Sofie—"

"It wasn't entirely his fault." It felt strange defending him after making him the villain in her head for so long. Strange, but right. "We had a misunderstanding. He didn't know about Sofie, but he does now and he's…trying."

"Is that what this is?" JoJo nodded to the present Rachel was fidgeting with. "Him trying?"

"I'm not sure what this is," she admitted, not just meaning the present.

"Well, open it," JoJo demanded impatiently. "I want to know what kind of bling the hot ballplayer sends his baby mama."

If she'd said it was private, JoJo would have instantly

accepted that and returned to her desk. She knew that. But somehow opening the present alone seemed like a much more intimidating prospect than doing it with a cheering section.

The wrapping was so flawless she was sure it had been professionally done. She couldn't picture Cam neatly creasing the corners. The box was a simple shirt box with no logo to provide a hint of what was inside. She pulled open the top, holding her breath for something ridiculously frivolous—a diamond tiara, a silk shawl—and when she pushed back the tissue paper a laugh burst out of her mouth.

It was a Christmas sweater. Quite possibly the world's ugliest Christmas sweater. Red and green striped, with a sequin Rudolph with a disproportionately huge nose.

"Huh." JoJo frowned as Rachel pulled the sweater from the box. Then she studied Rachel's face and started to smile. "Good present."

Rachel's brow knit in confusion at JoJo's reaction. "What? It's hideous." A tiny matching Sofie-sized sweater lay among the tissue paper.

"Yeah. And you love it." JoJo grinned knowingly, retreating back toward her desk. "Merry Christmas, Mama."

Rachel frowned after her. Then glanced down at the ridiculous sweater as her cell phone rang—and Cam's name appeared on the screen.

"Do you like it?" he asked as soon as she'd said hello. "I dropped it off fifteen minutes ago. Don't tell me you haven't opened it."

"I might have been waiting for Christmas. That is the traditional thing to do."

"But you didn't." She could hear the smile in his

voice. "Isn't it awful? The nose lights up."

She snorted. "Of course it does." She couldn't suppress her smile. It was just so *ugly*.

"I figure everyone needs a hideous Christmas sweater. It's required. And I might have ulterior motives."

Her stomach clenched on those words. "You do?"

"My parents have a tradition. Ugly sweater caroling followed by cookies and cocoa. Tomorrow night." She heard the hesitation in his voice. "I was hoping you and Sofie might join us. There are ugly sweaters in it for your mother and Yaya if they want to come too."

She bit her lip. "I don't know what their plans are, but I do know none of us can carry a tune."

"You can't be any worse than Carly. We're more about enthusiasm than talent. Will you come? I promise the cocoa makes up for the auditory assault."

"I..." God, she was being ridiculous. It was just caroling. Both of their families would be there. She forced lightness she didn't feel into her voice. "How can I resist an invitation like that? I'll see if Mom and Yaya are free, but Sofie and I are in."

"Excellent! Carly's hosting, because she's an insufferable control freak. The festivities technically start around six, but everyone is always late—and don't worry about eating before you come. There will be food everywhere, and not just cookies and cocoa."

"It sounds very festive," she murmured, nerves starting to whisper through her.

"It is. Do you want me to pick you up?"

"No. No, we'll make our own way."

"I can't wait to see you," Cam said, with a little extra rasp to his voice, and Rachel shivered.

She told herself she *definitely* wasn't still feeling the

effects of that voice when she refocused on the seating chart, her face flushed from a silly Christmas sweater.

The Russell House event was on track. Her Christmas shopping was in hand, the decorations were up, and she was going caroling tonight—but none of that was what had her blushing over a sweater. It was Cam. And she couldn't let herself get in too deep.

* * * * *

Cam had told her his family was big. She just hadn't realized exactly how big. Or been prepared for the sheer volume that many people could produce, the wall of sound hitting her as soon as she walked in the door.

Cam appeared instantly at her side, grinning broadly and wearing the same awful reindeer sweater he'd sent her—though it looked entirely too good on him. "You made it!" He dropped a kiss on Sofie's head. "Welcome to the insanity."

Rachel had a moment to worry that the sweater was some kind of couple thing, before she noticed that everyone was wearing the same horrendous reindeer sweater—which made it that much harder to tell everyone apart and figure out exactly how many children were racing around excitedly.

"Come on. I'll introduce you to everyone." Cam put his hand on the small of her back, ushering her into the room as his parents greeted her mother and Yaya, introducing them around. She tried not to fixate on that hand on her back—even when every member of his family was definitely noticing it.

Rachel gave up on remembering names almost immediately, focusing on learning who belonged to whom instead. Carly's husband Eddie—the only name she got before the sheer number of them overwhelmed her—had thinning blond hair, a beer gut, and a loud laugh that seemed to echo in the room. Shelby's husband was a tall man with midnight skin, a soft accent and dry sense of humor, largely silent until he lobbed a sarcastic remark into the fray, while Ashley's husband filled any silence with his energy. He was barely taller than his wife—and a full head shorter than Rachel—but still seemed to be everywhere, a slim, Korean whirling dervish weaving in and out between children. And there were a *lot* of children.

But what struck Rachel most about the entire scene was how they played off one another. These people knew one another. As everyone got ready to head outside, they laughed together, they teased one another, and they all moved automatically to help the little one who lost a glove or defuse growing arguments between the kids about who knew the most carols. It was a family. A big, noisy, overwhelming family.

And they'd welcomed her easily into the fold. Though she didn't feel easy. The panic-rabbits were frantic in her brain.

Cam had sent over sweaters for Yaya and her mother as well, so at least they looked like they belonged as they were surrounded by Cam's family. Apparently a new sweater, worse each year than the last, was a crucial part of the tradition.

"The matching sweaters will be the only harmonious thing about us," one of Cam's brothers-in-law joked.

He wasn't wrong, she learned as soon as everyone had piled on coats and ventured out into the evening to serenade the neighbors. Theirs was the kind of caroling that got by on gusto rather than talent—but if the laughter was nearly as loud as the singing, no one seemed to mind.

Sofie was delighted by all her cousins, chasing after

them on her chubby little toddler legs, looking like a pink marshmallow in her snowsuit. The older ones were obviously used to little kids, stopping to help her and making sure she wasn't left out. Rachel watched her like a hawk, but Sofie wasn't the one having a hard time adjusting to this new normal.

Andie was laughing with Cam's sisters, Yaya was teaching some of the older kids the Greek words to *Silent Night*. It was only Rachel who couldn't seem to relax. Especially when Cam returned to her side.

She didn't know how to behave, didn't know who she was supposed to be. She and Cam weren't really together, but his family seemed to have absorbed hers into it as if they were—and it felt like they were all watching her, some curious, some cautious.

"You okay?" Cam asked as they wandered en masse to the third house they would be serenading. "You've been awfully quiet."

"Trust me, you don't want me singing any louder than this."

He smiled, but his eyes were serious. "I didn't mean the singing. I'm sorry if this is overwhelming. I know we can be a lot."

"No, your family's great."

"But?"

But I don't know where I fit in. I don't know what we are to each other right now, or what I want us to be and even if I did know you're leaving in a few months to go back to LA.

But she couldn't say any of that. The panic-bunnies in her mind scrambled frantically for an answer.

A snowball flew through the air, smacking Cam in the chest and, thankfully, distracting him. He spun toward the culprit, roaring and charging toward his nieces and nephews, who screamed and scattered.

Rachel watched him scoop Sofie up, tucking her against his chest as he ran, and her own chest got tight.

"He's so happy you're here."

Rachel turned toward the voice, Cam's mother appearing at her side. "It was nice of you all to include us."

"You're family now," she said simply. "And I think you're going to be good for him."

Was his ex good for him? It was the kind of thing she'd wanted to ask ever since she'd learned he was married. The divorce hadn't been his call. Was he really over her? But Rachel was scared of how much it would reveal about how she was feeling about Cam if she asked.

Cam handed Sofie off to Carly and tumbled to the ground beneath a pile of kids, groaning dramatically. His mother smiled, watching him. "Try not to hurt him," she requested softly, her eyes still on her son. "I know he seems like a tough guy and he's always trying to prove to everyone that he's okay, but he's a softie underneath. He takes things to heart—he always has. So be careful with him, okay? You can hurt him more than you know."

One of her grandchildren flung himself against her legs and she bent down, laughing, allowing herself to be pulled away into the fray, leaving Rachel alone with the echoes of her words. She seemed to think Rachel had all the power. That *Cam* was the one in danger of getting hurt.

She hadn't thought about his vulnerability. Only her own. She'd been pushing him away. Keeping him at a distance.

Her mother's laughter rang across the lawn and Rachel looked over to see her dodging snowballs. Yaya and Sofie and her mother all seemed to have integrated so easily into Cam's family, but Rachel had been holding herself back all night. All week for that matter. Keeping a piece of herself safely removed from him. Scared to play his game.

She was a worrier. She borrowed trouble from the future and couldn't seem to let go of the baggage of the past, but she *wanted* to be more like her mother. She wanted to be able to make the best. She wanted to be able to enjoy this—even if this life and this family hadn't been part of her original plan.

But how did she do that?

Rachel crouched down, scooping up a handful of snow and calmly packing it into a ball. The snowball fight had swelled to include most of the family, but no one had noticed her on the fringes. She wound up, took aim, and threw her snowball as hard as she could.

It bounced off Cam's shoulder with an unimpressive puff.

But the pathetic impact had Cam turning to track down the source. When he spotted her, a slow, wicked grin spread across his face. "Oh, you are gonna regret that."

Rachel squeaked and turned to run, realizing too late that she'd just instigated a snowball fight with a man who *threw snowball-shaped things for a freaking living*. She wove a zig-zagging route through his family, trying to avoid giving him a clear shot, but a quick glance back showed he'd given chase—and was gaining ground.

Note to self: don't provoke the professional athlete.

The snowball fight had spread, working its way back to Carly's house with some of the neighbors coming out to join the fray.

"Not near the cars!" Carly shouted to one of the kids—and Rachel saw her chance. If she could just make it to the driveway, Cam wouldn't risk missing her and hitting one of the fancy SUVs, not right after Carly had warned the kids away from them.

She took off in a sprint across the lawn, her boots sinking into the snow—

And something hard smacked into her from behind, lifting her off her feet. She squealed as she twisted in the air, Cam's arms firm around her as they tumbled into a snowbank. He took the brunt of the impact and she landed half on top of him, laughing and out-of-breath from running.

Snow puffed up into the air around them and his grey eyes glinted. His face was so close they were breathing one another's air—and suddenly she was breathless for a whole new reason.

"Cam…"

"Have I ever mentioned how gorgeous you are when you're covered in snow?" The extra rasp in his voice sent shivers streaking along her skin that had nothing to do with the cold. His gaze dropped to her lips.

"Cocoa time!"

Rachel jerked and shoved away from Cam at the shout from his mother. Scrambling to her feet, she glanced around to see if anyone else had noticed their moment in the snow. No one seemed to be watching, but she saw more than one hidden smile as the family trickled back toward the house.

"Come on, you two," Cam's mother called, smiling. "You can't miss cocoa. It's tradition."

"I swear my mother adds more 'long-standing' family traditions every year." Cam's gravelly voice was too close to her ear and Rachel sidled away. She'd wanted to move forward with Cam as co-parents, but she hadn't meant *this*. She needed to keep her distance and keep her head.

She spotted Sofie in Carly's arms and was reminded why she was really here. For the baby. "You're lucky," she said to Cam.

"I know." He smiled, his eyes warm, and Rachel couldn't hold his gaze, heat rising to her face.

Distance. She needed distance.

CHAPTER SIXTEEN

He should have kissed her when he had the chance.

Cam watched Rachel from across his sister's kitchen—which seemed to be as close as she was willing to get to him. Every time he edged closer, she circled the other direction.

All night he'd been trying not to pressure her, trying not to rush her, but when he'd had her in his arms in the snow it had hit him like a freight train. *This* was what he wanted. Not just Sofie as part of his family. Not just Rachel involved by extension as her mother. He wanted her as *his*. He wanted to be allowed to hold her. He wanted it all.

And she was just as relationship-shy as she'd ever been.

She might not have let him within ten feet of her if Sofie hadn't chosen that moment to burst into noisy tears. Cam was at the baby's side in an instant. She'd been at the kids table with the cousins, but now sat on the floor, a siren-wail of misery rising out of her mouth.

"What happened?" he demanded of the other kids, gathering Sofie into his arms as she continued to sob. "Did she fall?"

"She wanted Ava's cookie," his oldest niece reported. Cam frowned, trying to connect the dots from wanting a cookie to on-the-floor-in-agony.

"That's a tired cry," Carly said with utmost Mom Authority as Rachel reached his side.

"Sorry about this," Rachel murmured, reaching for the baby, her face flushed with embarrassment. Sofie resisted, clinging to Cam like a bur. "It's almost her bedtime and there's been so much excitement."

"We all get it," Carly assured her—though Cam was still trying to mentally adjust from panic-that-Sofie-was-hurt to Sofie's-just-pitching-a-fit. "Do you want to put her down in the guest room?"

Sofie's hiccupping sobs crescendoed. Cam bounced her, murmuring soothing nonsense, and Rachel cringed. "It might be best if we just go." With one hand on Sofie's back, she glanced toward her mother and grandmother, clearly reluctant to drag them away when they were having a good time.

"I'll drive you," Cam offered. "That way your mother and Yaya can stay as long as they like."

"No, really, it's fine—" Rachel said, at the same moment her mother—who had apparently been listening in—exclaimed, "Oh, would you? That's so sweet."

Rachel shot her mother a death glare, but Cam sidled between them before she could argue. "It's no trouble. I want to." He wanted to spend more time with Sofie and Rachel—but he also wanted to show her that he was in this. That he wanted to be fifty percent responsible for all of it—even the toddler tantrums. "Not just the Fun Dad, remember?"

Reluctance was visible in every line of Rachel's body, but Sofie chose that moment to go into another siren wail and Rachel caved. "Thank you. I'll just say my goodbyes."

Cam was already moving. "I'll meet you out front."

"Take my car." Carly followed him out of the kitchen, pressing her keys into his hand. "It has a car seat."

A car seat. Right. He was going to need to get one of those for the Range Rover.

"And don't put her in her snowsuit," Carly told him. "Poofy winter coats interfere with the car seat straps—just put her under your coat to keep her warm until you get her buckled in."

"Right," Cam mumbled, realizing again how unprepared he was for this.

"Good luck," Carly called, the phrase loaded with meaning he couldn't unravel with Sofie wailing in his ear.

The screaming 'no' chorus kicked into gear the second he stepped into the foyer. Putting on a coat while holding a flailing child wasn't a skill he'd ever suspected he was going to need, but he was becoming an expert tonight. He wrapped his coat around Sofie as Carly had told him, holding it closed around the baby as Rachel joined them.

They stepped out into the snow—and he saw the flaw in their plan. Carly was blocked in.

"Let's take your car," he suggested. "Mine doesn't have a car seat yet and Carly's is blocked in. I'll leave my keys for your mom and Yaya."

"But then how will you get home?"

"I'll get an Uber home and come pick it up tomorrow. I'll trade the keys while you load her in—" But when he tried to hand Sofie to her mother, she screeched and clung to Cam.

"She probably doesn't even remember what she's upset about," Rachel said.

"Okay, new plan. You exchange keys. I'll load her

in."

Rachel nodded, jogging back into the house—and he experienced a tiny, momentary thrill that they were working together, like a real team. Until Sofie screamed again. He'd only managed to get half of Sofie's resisting arms and legs into the car seat straps by the time Rachel returned and took over. She slapped the keys into his palm. "Warm up the car," she demanded, yanking at the car seat straps with expert movements.

Cam was nothing if not good at following directions. He had the engine running and his seat adjusted by the time Rachel closed the door. She leapt into the passenger seat and he pulled out as she was buckling her seatbelt.

*****

Rachel cringed as Cam took the corner out of the neighborhood and Sofie kicked into another round of wails, the sound gouging at her heart like it always did. She *knew* Sofie was just exhausted and fighting it, but those cries just killed her. You'd think she'd be used to it by now, but it never seemed to magically get easier.

It was a testament to how distracted she was that it wasn't until they were five minutes down the road and the baby finally quieted that Rachel realized Cam didn't need to be there. If he was only driving her to take an Uber back…

"I could have driven myself." She didn't need to be spending any more time alone with Cam, feeling any closer to him.

Cam barely glanced her way, his attention on the road. "I wanted to do it. Seemed like you could use a hand and she's my kid too. I'm fifty percent responsible for those impressive lungs."

Said lungs were now breathing quietly as Sofie slept in the backseat and Rachel stared out the passenger window, trying to figure out why it felt so different when Cam helped as opposed to when Yaya or her mother stepped in. She knew they didn't mind, she'd heard them say it a thousand times, but she always felt like she had to apologize. But this time, with Cam…it had felt like he belonged here. Like they were in it together, like she didn't have to feel bad that he was taking some of the burden off her shoulders. And that was a dangerous thing to be thinking. Especially when she had no idea if he planned to stay.

"I'm sorry we had to leave so early," she said, focusing on the present instead of the uncertain future. "Thank you for inviting us tonight. I want Sofie to have those kinds of connections. A big family. You're lucky to have them."

"They are pretty great. Doesn't mean they aren't also obnoxious. Shelby especially seems to get into the most ridiculous feuds with people. But we still love each other like crazy."

"I always wished for a big family. When I was little," Rachel admitted. "I don't think it occurred to me how loud it would be."

He laughed, silencing the sound abruptly with a hasty glance in the mirror to see if he'd disturbed Sofie, but the baby slept on. "We certainly don't lack for volume." He kept his eyes on the road ahead, asking oh-so-casually, "So you want a bunch more kids?"

"I…" Rachel's mouth went dry. In theory, she'd wanted a big family—lots of kids, lots of noise. In practice, she'd figured Sofie would be her one and only. It took two to make siblings, and she hadn't planned on letting another man into her life any time soon. And she didn't have the financial resources to have more kids on her own. But she couldn't say any of that to Cam. The words twisted around in her brain, tangling before they got to her tongue.

"I always wanted a bunch of kids," he commented, taking mercy on her after the awkward silence. "Well, not always. I didn't really start thinking about it until my sisters and teammates starting having them and I realized I wanted that too." He grimaced. "Slow study."

"Did you and your wife ever…?"

"Erika didn't want kids. And I wasn't always very good at listening to her when she tried to tell me that. It took her leaving to really drive it home."

"So she left you?" He'd said that before, but she hadn't really processed it. It was hard to fit the puzzle pieces of the truth into the picture she'd built out of her assumptions.

"Same day she got diagnosed. At the time it felt like the worst failure, but now I see it was for the best. She's even sort of indirectly the reason I found you again."

Rachel shook her head. "What do you mean?"

"Russell House. She's the reason I got involved with them. They were amazing throughout her treatment. Any way I can support them, I will."

Rachel tried not to fixate on the warmth in his voice when he talked about the charity. When he talked about his ex. Did he still have feelings for her? That soft fondness wasn't the sound of someone who was over her.

"How's the fundraiser stuff going?" he asked. "Any more wine deliveries?"

"No, the mystery bags are all packed and ready to go to the venue. In fact everything's going so well it's making me nervous."

"It could just be a sign that you're prepared for anything."

"I hope so. I really need it go well." She fidgeted with a button on her coat, the loose one that Sofie always played with while she was strapping her into her car seat. "It's my first time being in charge of an event of this size, and I just want to prove to my boss that I can do this."

"Of course you can. You're the most organized person I know. Pathologically organized. She has to know that."

"It's not just about organization. Yes, I want everything to run smoothly, but we also want everyone to have a good time—and to make a lot of money for the charity. To show they were smart to go to the expense of hiring us and made exponentially more than they would have if they'd just used volunteers. It's my reputation, and TD Events' reputation, and the Russell House's financial future on the line. Everything has to be perfect."

"You realize most people won't notice if things aren't up to your standards of perfection."

"Yes, but *I* will."

"I can't argue with that." He glanced over at her as he pulled into her apartment complex. "I don't suppose you have any time in your airtight schedule this weekend? I have some Christmas presents that need wrapping and I thought maybe you and Sofie might want to come over and help. I'll provide dinner."

"Um…" Saying no was on the tip of her tongue. She wasn't even sure why, just that a little distance felt like the safest choice. To stall for time, she climbed out of the car and began unloading Sofie.

Cam came around behind her, jingling the keys in his hand. "I promise I'm not just asking so I can get you to wrap my presents for me. I'm actually amazing at gift-wrapping. Seriously. World class."

Rachel cocked her head at him. "Then why do you need my help?"

"I don't. I just want to see you."

He said it so simply, as if it was the most natural thing in the world. How did he do that? How did he unravel all her defenses against him with six simple words?

"I'll check my schedule."

Cam grinned. He nodded to the carrier in her arms. "Do you want a hand getting her settled?"

She glanced down at the limp baby. "No. She probably won't even wake up when I transfer her. Thanks for driving me back." It hadn't been necessary—but she was starting to realize that the unnecessary things were sometimes kind of nice.

"Any time. G'night, Rachel."

She nodded her goodbye, starting up the stairs to her apartment, and trying to figure out just when Cam had started feeling like such a necessary unnecessary thing.

CHAPTER SEVENTEEN

He still had the same condo.

The three-story townhome had to be four thousand square feet—all of it light and bright and luxurious. The natural colors and textures of Boulder's rustic mountain esthetic paired with modern angles and lines like a jigsaw puzzle. It was gorgeous. And too familiar.

Rachel had been so sure he would have sold it when he moved to LA, until she pulled up to the address Cam had texted her on Saturday night. The same place she'd spent those September nights with him, where he'd told her he loved her.

But when he opened the front door she saw how much it had changed.

There was a high chair at the end of the butcher block table and an empty box for a car seat lying on its side near the island. The room smelled of pine, a ten-foot tree dominating one corner. There were a handful of presents beneath it already—including one large enough to fit an entire person inside it, which she was sure held the stuffed animal he'd texted her a picture of when he bought it from Costco—but it was the highchair Rachel's gaze kept returning to.

She arched a brow at the baby debris. "You've been busy."

"I have." He grinned. "Come on in. Hello, sweet

girl!"

"Da!" It wasn't quite "Daddy" but it made Rachel's heart jump as Sofie lurched sideways in her arms, flinging herself toward him. Cam caught her, lifting her up above his head and spinning in circles until her giggles filled the room.

Rachel set Sofie's diaper bag near the door, toeing off her boots and shrugging out of her coat. Cam turned toward her with Sofie perched high in his arms.

"My sisters helped. They couldn't wait to tell me what to do when I told them I wanted to make this place Sofie-friendly." He nudged the car seat box out of the way with his foot. "I didn't quite finish cleaning up, but Ashley said Sofie would probably love playing with the box."

"She probably will."

"Wait until you see the rest of it. There's a whole nursery set up. Well. Mostly set up."

He led the way down a hallway she didn't think she'd ever noticed when she'd visited him here two years ago—and why would she have? The master was upstairs and she'd barely been aware of anything but Cam's bedroom. And the rooftop hot tub.

The nursery, as Cam had called it, was bigger than the room Rachel shared with Sofie now—and it was adorable. His sisters had outdone themselves. Crib, changing table, a rocking chair with a little bookcase displaying dozens of books. New books with shiny, unbroken spines—not the used ones that were barely holding together that she'd been reading Sofie.

"What do you think, Sofie?" Cam asked, setting her down so she could explore the blocks and stuffed animals on a little play mat.

It was exactly the kind of nursery Rachel would have

wanted—and she wasn't sure how to feel. Delighted that Sofie got to have a place like this? Jealous that Cam was the one to give it to her? Grateful? Hesitant?

Even if he was playing at being a dad now, even if he was trying so hard to do everything right, at some point he would have to go back to LA. She shouldn't get used to having him around. This wasn't the new reality. It was just another phase to get used to—and it would pass as quickly as all of Sofie's phases seemed to pass.

She couldn't let herself get used to him.

She cleared her throat roughly. "You said you had presents to wrap?"

*****

He'd bought her a tape dispenser.

She'd brought the crate of wrapping supplies from her storage unit—tissue paper, wrapping paper, ribbons, bows, tags—and she hadn't needed any of it. Cam had a fully stocked area set up in the basement game room, flawlessly organized and ready to go, but then he'd handed her a little tape dispenser that she could strap to the back of her hand.

"To make wrapping more efficient," he'd said. And she'd just about melted.

It was a silly thing to get gooey over, but there it was.

He really was amazing at wrapping presents. Which shouldn't have surprised her. He'd always been good with his hands.

Yet another thing she had to keep reminding herself not to think.

He'd even been able to wrap presents with Sofie sitting on his lap "helping"—which was a miracle in itself. The baby had since fallen asleep on the couch and Cam had carried her into the nursery. Rachel knew she should be getting her home and into her own bed, but she'd been having such a good time she hadn't wanted to stop. And the packages really did need wrapping. At least that was the excuse she gave herself.

It was *fun*. Being here with him. Talking about anything and everything with Christmas music playing in the background and Sofie snoozing peacefully on the baby monitor. Instead of feeling her usual surge of satisfaction at a task completed, Rachel was actually a little disappointed when the last present was wrapped.

The night had been so *easy*. So relaxing. She couldn't remember the last time she could say that. And she wasn't ready for it to end. But good sense had her gathering up the packages she'd brought over to wrap.

"You don't have to go," Cam offered softly, echoing her thoughts.

"I should get Sofie home."

"You could stay here." When she went still, he added, "There's another guest room, right next to Sofie's. It's yours if you want it. Any time you like."

But she didn't want the guest room. And she wasn't sure she would sleep there if she stayed. Which was why she needed to go.

"I have to work tomorrow. Our whole routine will be out of whack if Sofie wakes up here. And neither of us have any pajamas."

"Pajamas." Cam nodded. "I'll have to get her some of those. Anything else I should add to the list?"

"You don't have to do all this. I can bring you a few of her things for when she stays over." The idea didn't sound nearly as terrifying as it had a few days ago. When had she started letting herself trust Cam with her baby?

"I want to," he insisted. "I like shopping for her. Making a place for you guys here."

A question had been whispering through the back of her mind all night and she finally let herself ask it. "Is this where you lived with Erika when you were married?"

If the question surprised him, he didn't show it. "No. We had a place down in Denver, near the ballpark. It was in a high rise. Great views, but I missed Boulder. When we split up, initially she went to live with her sister and I stayed in the apartment, but it just felt cold there by myself. I decided I'd rather have a forty minute commute and be close to home so I gave Erika the apartment and got this place. I'd only been in it a few months when we met."

"And you kept it when you moved to LA?"

"I knew I wanted to spend the off-seasons here. I've never wanted to put down roots anywhere else. And I didn't want to get too confident that I was going to stay in LA. Buying a house is a good way to get traded. Or kicked back down to the minors."

"Still superstitious, I see."

His grin was wry as he leaned against the covered pool table they'd used as a wrapping station. "Never trust the good things to last. That's my motto."

She blinked. The words seemed to apply to more than just baseball, but she just asked, "Are most teams in the habit of sending All-Star catchers down to the minors?"

"It happens more often than you might think. I only made the All-Star team once, three years ago. And yeah, I'm a franchise player now, but all it takes is one slump to change that. Everyone's watching, waiting to see when I'll lose a step and be too old to get it back."

"You're what? Thirty? Downright ancient." The way he leaned against the pool table, the muscles beneath his shirt relaxed but still bulging impressively in all the right places, made it hard to think of him as anything close to retirement age.

"Catching is hard on your body. Some guys do it until they're forty, but most of us are put out to pasture way before that. All it takes is me pulling a muscle at a moment when they have a catcher down in Triple-A who's on a hot streak and my position's gonna go to some kid. It's only luck that's keeping me here."

"Luck. So you haven't been training in the off season?"

"Of course I train. I work out every day. Run drills a few times a week. You gotta stay sharp."

"Uh-huh." Rachel cocked her head. "The way you define 'luck' it sounds a lot like working harder than anyone else. You know it's not random that you made it to the majors. You earned it."

"Yeah, but the second you start to believe you earned your place, the second you get comfortable, that's when the rug gets yanked out. You can't afford to take your foot off the gas. Not for a second."

"That sounds exhausting."

"It's just focus. Staying on top is like walking a tightrope. It's easy to fall at any moment if you lose your concentration. So you learn to stay sharp."

"And what happens if you fall?"

She'd meant fall off the pedestal he'd worked so hard to keep himself on, but when he met her eyes something shifted in the air. "I don't know," he murmured, and suddenly it didn't feel like they were talking about baseball anymore.

She swallowed, looking away from the sudden heat in his eyes, and her gaze landed on the baby monitor. "I should get Sofie home."

It was obvious she was grasping for excuses, running like a coward, but Cam let her get away with it. He straightened from his boneless lean against the table and jerked his chin toward the pile of presents she'd gathered up. "I can bring those over to you tomorrow so you don't have to mess with them tonight."

"Great. That'd be great. Thanks." Everything had been so easy a few minutes ago, but now awkwardness was wriggling and creeping beneath her skin.

She turned and led the way up the stairs to the room where Sofie slept. She looked so peaceful Rachel hesitated to disturb her, but if she stayed she knew she would do something she would regret.

Cam lifted Sofie, who stayed boneless and limp, onto his shoulder. He wordlessly followed Rachel to the front door.

She was suddenly self-conscious of her fuzzy Christmas tree socks as she slid her feet into her boots. Too aware of her arms as she shoved them into the sleeves of her coat. Her body didn't feel like hers anymore. Too heavy and too awkward.

She turned to Cam, ready to relieve him of Sofie, but he wasn't looking at her. His head was tipped up, staring at something on the ceiling. Rachel followed his gaze and felt her face begin to heat.

Mistletoe. Of course.

She lowered her gaze from the treacherous plant. Cam was watching her now, a gleam in his eyes. She narrowed hers. "Did you plan this?"

"Me?" He kept his protestation of innocence as quiet as she'd kept her question, both of them whispering to avoid disturbing the baby. "I'm the spontaneous one, remember? You're the planner."

For a second she actually thought he was telling the

truth, that he'd been entirely unaware of the mistletoe over his entryway—his sisters had helped him decorate, after all—but then she caught the glint in his eye. "You're impossible."

His eyes softened as he stepped toward her, Sofie still zonked out on his shoulder. "Are you going to flaunt tradition?"

"Cam..." He leaned closer—and she stopped him with a hand on his chest, ducking her chin. He instantly went still beneath her hand, not pushing. "For two years I've been telling myself I was wrong to fall for you," she whispered to his sternum.

Cam's chest rose beneath her splayed hand as he inhaled. "There's always going to be a risk, Rachel. There's always going to be a possibility things will go south. But you don't let the fear of striking out stop you from stepping into the batter's box."

"I do," she whispered. "I always have. Except with you."

"Then maybe it's time to get back in the game."

She lifted her chin. Her eyes were the last thing she raised, shielded by her lashes until the last moment when she looked up at him—and knew this kiss would have nothing to do with the mistletoe, and everything to do with how much she'd missed him.

She'd hated herself for missing him. Kicked herself for the piece of her that hadn't been able to let him go. But now she curled her fingers in his shirt, tugging him closer, and his lips quirked up in that cocky grin and that longing inside her she'd been trying to smother came back to life.

God, she'd missed him.

His lips touched hers. Soft. Lingering. A sweet, stretching taffy moment that was all anticipation and hope. Once. Then again.

The third kiss settled in for a nice long visit, their lips reacquainting themselves with one another after far too long. It wasn't heat and passion and momentum—it would have been easier if it was. This was something else. Not just chemistry. Emotion. Things she'd told herself she wasn't going to let herself feel for him again.

After several more minutes than she should have allowed herself, Rachel ducked her chin, breaking the kiss. Her face had grown hot, her breath quick. They still stood like statues beneath the mistletoe, her hand gripping his shirt, his loosely cupping her elbow while his other arm supported their daughter— Sofie still passed out hard on his shoulder.

"I should go," she whispered without looking up.

His fingers flexed on her elbow, but other than that he remained motionless. "You could stay." His already gravelly voice was even deeper than usual.

Still looking down, Rachel shook her head, just once, side-to-side, and Cam's hand fell away. She forced herself to release his shirt, pulling her hand back and hugging it against her stomach.

"It's okay," his rough voice assured her. "We've got time."

Except it didn't feel like they did. The Russell House fundraiser was in less than a week. Then Christmas, a few days later. New Year's…January...then she would blink and he'd be leaving for Spring Training.

She couldn't let herself fall for him again. For Sofie's sake. She had to be smart.

But what if this could work? A little voice whispered beneath cold hard logic. *What if being with him is the smart thing?* They could live happily-ever-after. Sofie could have both her parents together. This could be forever.

But she couldn't let herself trust that. Not yet. So she took her daughter from his arms and headed home.

CHAPTER EIGHTEEN

He had time. Cam kept repeating that to himself over and over again.

Don't push this. Don't rush. You have time.

But he'd never been good at letting up.

He pushed. He worked at things harder than anyone else. That was how a kid who'd gotten cut from his high school baseball team had made it to the majors. But he couldn't push Rachel. He didn't want to screw this up. So he needed to learn some patience. Even if it was the last thing he wanted to do.

Things had been good the last week. Not as good as he'd like them to be, but good.

They hadn't kissed again, but he'd seen Rachel and Sofie every day. They were both getting more comfortable with him. Sofie called him "Da" all the time now—which never failed to make his throat tight. Rachel had stopped watching him like a hawk every time he picked Sofie up. He didn't think she'd known she was doing it in the first place, but he'd definitely noticed when she started trusting him with her.

It felt like they could actually be a family—but he knew there was still a chance it could all blow up in his face. Life had a tendency to do that right when he let himself believe he was going to get what he wanted.

But still, he was optimistic.

The Russell House event was tomorrow night—and it felt weird to be thinking about being auctioned off as a bachelor when he felt completely off-the-market. They hadn't slept together. They weren't even technically back together, but he was hers. Completely. Just like he had been last time right before it fell apart.

He felt like he was ahead in the game, but there was still a chance for fate to come back in the ninth inning and knock him on his ass. He needed some insurance runs, to put some comfortable distance between himself and the karmic ass-kicking he was afraid was coming for him.

That was what tonight was all about. Just him and Rachel. No baby. No distractions. No evasions.

It was a minor miracle he'd managed to talk her into taking the night before the fundraiser off. Only the fact that she literally hadn't been able to think of anything else to do to prepare had gotten him this date.

His parents were watching Sofie. The two of them were over-the-moon at the chance to spend more time with their new granddaughter, though both of them had very carefully avoided commenting on the fact that Cam was taking Rachel out. His family had developed an unprecedented sense of tact this week. No one had teased him, or Rachel when they saw her. They all seemed like they were holding their breath—waiting to see how it would turn out.

And all he could do was hope like hell that he didn't screw it up.

Rachel met him at his place. His parents were already there, waiting to stay with Sofie. Having them there, standing in the background smiling proudly felt weirdly like meeting up to go to Prom—if it hadn't been for the baby she was dropping off. Or the fact that no one going to Prom had ever looked as lethal in a little black dress as Rachel did.

Her hair was down, curling around her shoulders and reminding him of that September.

She gave his parents a list of instructions on Sofie's care—as if they hadn't managed to raise four kids and approximately twelve-dozen grandkids. She probably would have stood there all night if Cam hadn't used their reservation time and her horror of being late to get her out the door.

She was quiet as they walked to his car and he held the door for her. He couldn't think of the right thing to say as he started toward the restaurant. Silence filled the car, an unwelcome tagalong. He'd never had trouble finding the right words in the past—but he'd also never cared this much about not screwing up.

The restaurant was crowded—unsurprising on a Friday night, especially around the holidays—and the noise covered some of their awkwardness though their conversation seemed limited to small talk. "I've heard this place is really good" and a joke about the cook taking out a vendetta on "The Twelve Days of Christmas" with his partridge special kept them from complete silence until the wine arrived.

He took a sip, watching Rachel do the same, and grimaced. "This is awful, isn't it?"

"The wine?" she asked, confused.

"No. This." He waved between them. "It's like I forgot how to talk to you."

Relief washed over her face now that he'd called out the elephant in the room. "I feel like we never used to be this awkward."

It might be the first time she'd willingly brought up their relationship from that golden September—that had to be a good sign, didn't it? "We weren't," he assured her. "We could talk for days. That first night, what was it? Three a.m. before we realized the party had ended and we were still talking on the balcony? I didn't get nearly enough sleep that entire month because we never stopped talking—it's amazing my play didn't suffer."

"I seem to remember you telling me you were having the best month of your career."

"I was. Or close to it. I probably owe you my signing bonus." He raised his wine glass to her. "My good luck charm."

She shook her head. "You keep blaming luck, but that isn't why you succeed."

"Maybe. But if I take credit for the success, then when the failure comes that's on me too. It's easier to take if it's all luck and there's nothing I can do but enjoy what I've been given."

"But you haven't been given it. You earned it."

He shrugged. "Lots of people work hard and they don't get where I am. Trust me, luck is part of it. I've seen that first hand."

She cocked her head, eyeing him over her wine glass. "There's a story there."

"Did I ever tell you about the time I got cut from my high school baseball team?" he asked, even though he knew he hadn't. He didn't talk about his failures. He had an image to protect and that image didn't include a time when Cameron Cole had ever been less than amazing at baseball.

"I don't think so." Rachel leaned forward, setting her glass on the table. "What happened?"

"I wasn't the star back then," he explained, fidgeting with the stem of his own glass. "I hit my growth spurt late and in high school I was still this scrawny kid, but I loved the game and I worked harder than anyone else on the team. My senior year I finally made varsity—barely. I'm not sure whether it was because the coaches took pity on me or there just weren't any better options for my position, but it wasn't because I was some six-foot-four natural jacking homers out of the park in every at bat."

Cam didn't tell this story often, but when he did this was when people always interrupted him. Telling him they couldn't believe there'd ever been a time when he wasn't amazing. Telling him they were sure he was much better than he was making himself out to be. But Rachel simply watched him, accepting him at his word.

"We were having a good run," he went on. "We had some great pitchers that year and we were on track to make it into the State Championships. Then, right toward the end of the season, a new kid moved to town. A six-foot-four natural, jacking homers in every at bat. And he'd played catcher at his last school."

Rachel cringed.

"Yeah. You can see where this is going. I was benched. I still played some—he missed practices and even a couple of games, but when he was there, he was in the line-up and I was watching from the dugout. Man, I hated him. I'm sure he was a nice guy—not his fault his parents moved in the middle of the year—but all I could see was that he'd stolen what I'd worked for. The coaches kept saying it wasn't about talent, it was about the team. It was about who worked hard and put in the hours and showed they wanted it the most. But when it was time to go to State and they had to pick their roster, they picked the natural, the kid who'd been skipping practices, but still made it look easy every time he swung the bat. I wasn't even surprised that I wasn't going to start, but I thought for sure I'd go as a back-up. But there were other kids who could back-up multiple positions and they wanted to bring an extra pitcher. So I was out. Not even on the bus."

Rachel cringed. "Ouch."

"Yep. We lost. And I was so certain at the time that if I had been there, we would have won. Like I could have lifted the team up on my shoulders and carried them to victory even though I'd never done it before. But that showed me it isn't about hard work. Those coaches believed in that kid and his natural talent more than they believed in my every day effort. So I worked my ass off to prove them wrong. When I hit my growth spurt right before college and bulked up, I started acting like it was easy for me. I worked out on my own, so my coaches and my teammates would see the results rather than the effort and think I was some phenom. And it worked. It pissed me off that it did, but people started treating me like I was a baseball god. I got drafted my junior year. I kept it up during my two years in the minors, all of my coaches blown away by how I didn't even have to work for it, and all of a sudden I was in the majors. It might have happened if I hadn't bullshitted everyone—people say it's all about the stats. Everyone's trying to Moneyball the game, but reputation matters. It's what convinces your coach to leave you in when you're in a slump rather than write you off. When you're in the line-up more regularly and getting more at bats, you get comfortable, you get a feel for the way people are pitching you, and your numbers go up."

"That isn't luck, though," Rachel argued. "That's strategy. You saw a way to improve your odds and you took it."

"Or I just tricked the world into thinking I was better

than I was."

Their food arrived then and Cam took the opportunity to let the subject drop, but Rachel waited until the waiter had departed and paused with her fork hovering over her scallops. "Has it occurred to you that maybe that other kid wasn't a natural either? That maybe there's no such thing and you're all trying to fool one another?"

"Maybe. It doesn't make it feel any less like I've been given something I don't deserve, and any second the universe is going to take it away from me. I'm always waiting for someone to figure out I'm a fraud."

Just like Rachel and Sofie. He'd gotten lucky, stupidly lucky, to have them back in his life. He'd screwed up before, by not telling her about Erika, and nearly lost his shot—and now that he had another one, he was waiting for the catch. Waiting for it all to go up in smoke.

"Okay, first off, you aren't a fraud. You really are amazing. And if it does go away...is that so horrible?" Rachel asked, and it took him a moment to recall they were talking about baseball. "You still have the experience, the memories. You've been in the majors for what? Almost a decade? How many people can say that?"

"I guess I'm just not ready for it to be over."

"Just don't be so worried about the ending that you forget to enjoy the present. At some point you're going to retire—whether it gets taken away from you or you let it go—but you're not going to be any less if you aren't playing baseball any more. You'll still be you."

He wasn't ready to talk about the future—baseball wasn't the thing he was most afraid of losing anymore, but he didn't want to scare Rachel off by pushing too hard. "That's good advice," he murmured, lifting his wine glass. "To the present."

A flush rose to Rachel's cheeks as she lifted her glass to gently ring against his. "To the present."

* * * * *

Rachel had never been very good at living in the present. She was a planner—which meant obsessively analyzing the future and making contingency plans for every possible outcome. But she was trying to follow her own advice tonight. She'd told Cam not to be so worried about the future that he forgot to enjoy the present and she was trying to do that—but worry kept sneaking in around the edges.

They were both quiet as Cam drove them back to his place. The tension that had been slowly building throughout the night loomed like a silent third passenger. He parked the Land Rover, coming around the hood to take her hand as they walked up the front walk toward the darkened condo. Sofie was asleep in the nursery and Rachel went to check on her as Cam thanked his parents and saw them out.

The baby was out cold, her little lashes resting so softly on her sweet cheeks. She always looked so angelic when she slept, her hair curling in every direction. His parents had put her in the little yellow footie pajamas Rachel had brought and she clutched Elmo in a death grip, even in sleep.

Distantly, Rachel heard the door open and close as Cam came back in after escorting his parents out. In theory, Rachel was only there to pick up the baby, but they both knew she wasn't going anywhere. This thing between them had been building since that mistletoe kiss, whispering in the background. She heard his footsteps approaching down the hall and met him at the doorway.

"Is everything okay?" he whispered, his eyes moving past her to touch on the baby.

How had they gotten here? Back in his condo with their daughter sleeping peacefully in the nursery? It felt like some surreal alternate reality where she'd never bumped into Erika at that game. Where Cam had told her about his soon-to-be-ex at some natural point in their relationship and she hadn't run. Where he'd been with her when she learned she was pregnant. With her through the anxiety and anticipation of those nine months. Holding her hand in the delivery room instead of her mom. There with her to hold their baby for the first time.

"I'm sorry," she whispered.

Cam shook his head, confused.

"I'm sorry we've missed this," she breathed—and kissed him.

In her sky high heels, they were almost the same height. All she had to do was lean forward and his lips were there, waiting for hers. The kiss started out as an apology—but that didn't last. Cam sank his hands into her hair, cupping her head, and need rushed over them like a tidal wave. She clutched his waist, leaning into him until their bodies pressed together and she could feel every line of him against every curve of her.

God, he felt good. She'd forgotten how good he felt. Tall and strong and firm. Steady. Like he could stand up to any force on earth.

They stumbled into the hallway, spinning so Rachel was the one with her back pressed against the far wall as Cam bent his knees and lifted her. Her tight skirt rode up as her legs went around his hips, the lethal heels crossed over his buttocks. She draped her arms around his neck, crossing her wrists the same way her ankles were crossed, as a sweet, drugging heat worked its way through her body.

She didn't know how long they kissed like that—like teenagers making out in a parked car, like they had all the time in the world. When the impatience got to be too much she ground her hips against his and Cam broke the kiss with a growl, hitching her up to carry her quickly through the house.

She bit her lip to hide her smile, ducking her head against his shoulder, holding on tight as he jogged up the stairs in an impressive display of athleticism. When they reached the master, he kicked the door closed and made a beeline for the bed, tossing her down on it.

Her hair had fallen around her face and she shoved it back. He towered over her, staring down at her like a conquering Viking. But instead of reaching for her, he reached for a small remote on the bedside table, pointing it in the general direction of the television. A tiny screen beside the television lit up. The baby monitor.

And Rachel freaking *melted*.

She didn't have to be the one who was thinking about Sofie all the time. He was thinking of her too. It was incredible the weight that took off her mind, the comfort of knowing she wasn't alone. Her mother and Yaya had always been there, but it was different. It was an imposition. Cam, he was in this with her. A team.

Though at this particular moment, she didn't want either of them thinking about Sofie.

"Come here." Her voice was husky even to her own ears, but Cam didn't seem to mind.

He braced his arms on either side of her, his eyes eating her up as he lowered himself over her. She had a little flicker of a moment to be self-conscious, to think of all the ways her body had changed since she had Sofie—but then he was kissing her neck, just below her jaw, his warm breath sending shivers over every inch of her skin, and she forgot to care about anything else.

He found the hidden side zipper on her dress, tugging the tight fabric over her head to reveal the matching red lace bra and panties. He cursed softly, his hands smoothing over her shoulders, her collarbones, trailing down her sternum until she needed him to *touch her already* or she was going to scream.

He'd shrugged out of his jacket, but she grabbed the collar of his button-down shirt and pulled him toward her roughly. "Stop messing around," she demanded with a hard kiss. "You don't know how long we have before she wakes up."

Cam laughed against her mouth. "What if I want to savor my Christmas present?" He traced a fingertip over red lace, making her arch.

"Savor faster," she insisted, making him laugh again—though he did at least develop a sense of urgency, yanking off his clothes, grinning and pressing kisses wherever he could reach as he threw aside each article.

Had there been this much laughter last time? Had things felt this natural? Like they belonged here, in each other's arms? She couldn't remember. She only knew this. *This* felt right.

It felt like forever.

CHAPTER NINETEEN

With a baby in the picture, morning afters had a very different feel. There was no lying in bed for hours, gazing at one another and making love over and over again while he professed his feelings.

Which was probably a damn good thing because if left to his own devices he probably would have told her he loved her again. And look how that had worked out last time. Sofie was the perfect distraction. Even if she did mean he woke up about two hours before his body thought was fair.

Rachel groaned and rolled onto her back, shoving her hair out of her face as the impatient, demanding cry came through the baby monitor.

"I'll get her," Cam offered, trying to work up the energy to actually heave himself out of bed.

One of Rachel's eyes cracked open. "Really?"

The hope in her voice gave him the motivation to actually lever himself into a sitting position and fling his legs over the side of the bed. "Sure. Go back to sleep."

She'd put on his shirt to pad to the bathroom in the middle of the night and it twisted around her as she turned toward him with a serious case of bedhead. It was a good look, a rumpled, sexy reminder of how they'd spent most of the night—making love and talking and making love again. But his daughter waited for no man, her crying taking on a frustrated note.

He pulled on his boxers and staggered barefoot through the house toward the impatient wail. It was still dark, but as he passed the grandfather clock he squinted at the face. A quarter to seven. He'd always thought of himself as a morning person—but apparently that only counted when morning didn't start before he was ready for it.

"Hey, baby girl," he said as he stepped into the nursery. Sofie's eyes locked onto him, but she kept up her why-have-I-been-waiting-so-long cries until the second he lifted her out of the crib. "Did you sleep well?" he asked, making idle conversation as he carried her to the changing table and got her a fresh diaper.

Sofie was wide awake, and by the time Cam was done changing her, he was too. The Russell House event was tonight and Rachel undoubtedly needed all the sleep she could get—something a selfless man would have thought of last night, though he couldn't regret the way they'd spent the midnight hours. All he could do was steal her a few more minutes now.

"Mama," Sofie demanded—she was a strong-willed little thing. All of her words had a distinct aura of command. Just like her mother.

"Mama's still sleeping. You wanna look at the Christmas tree?" It was one of Sofie's primary fascinations and she agreed instantly.

He carried her into the great room and over to the tree his sisters had helped him decorate, inhaling the pine scent. "Dow!" the little dictator in his arms demanded, emphasizing the order with a bounce.

"How do we ask nicely?" he said, echoing something he must have heard Rachel say five dozen times in the last week, and Sofie's whole demeanor instantly changed.

She smiled sweetly, actually fluttering her lashes, and chirped angelically, "Dow peez!"

"You're a con artist, you know that?" he said as he plopped her on her feet and she toddled toward the tree, patting the presents and chattering to herself.

"You know the funniest thing is happening to my tree," Rachel spoke from behind him.

"Mama!" Sofie shouted, running toward her mother, tripping on nothing, tumbling to her hands and knees and popping back up again to run some more.

Rachel—fully dressed now, though the dress from last night had a definite morning-after chic—met her halfway, scooping her up and giving her a kiss. "Good morning, Sofie Bear."

"I was trying to let you sleep in." He bent to claim his own good morning peck.

"We need to get going." But her gaze lingered gratifyingly on his bare chest. "Mom and Yaya will be wondering where we are."

Cam's eyebrows popped up. "I think they know."

She flushed, but didn't meet his eyes, pulling on her all-business demeanor as a shield. "Be that as it may, we still need to go. I have a lot to do today to get ready for the event tonight."

"Can I pick you up later? We can drive downtown together."

"No, I have to be there so much earlier than you do. You'd just be bored for hours."

"I could help," he offered.

"You're a guest," she insisted. "The guest of honor. Just go and have fun. You probably won't see much of me. I'll be busy all night."

"You'll have time for a dance, though, right?"

Sofie wriggled to be let down and Rachel set her on the ground. He caught her eye when she straightened and she averted her gaze, pressing a smile between her lips. "One dance," she promised, relenting. "After the auction. But you have to dance with the bidders too. We want them all to run up your price."

"It doesn't feel weird to you? That I'm selling myself to the highest bidder tonight?"

"Of course not." She smoothed a hand over his chest, as if she couldn't stop herself. "You're selling a baseball experience. The winner will probably be buying you for a kid in their life. Or it could easily be a man who wins."

"And if it's a woman?"

"Then you will give her an amazing day at the ball park, a day she will never forget." She smiled sweetly. "But if you so much as kiss her I will not be responsible for my actions."

He grinned, delighted by the flash of possessiveness. "Fair enough."

Rachel met his eyes as Sofie began patting the presents again—either admiring them or having a conversation with them, it was hard to tell which. "So we're doing this," she murmured, a flicker of uncertainty behind the words.

"We're doing this," he assured her, eliminating the space between them. He looped his arms around her, locking his hands at the small of her back and gently tugging her forward. "No regrets?"

He almost regretted asking, giving her the chance to back out—until she smiled and tipped her face up to his. "No regrets."

She wasn't in the heels anymore and had to go up on her tiptoes to kiss him. He bent his head, meeting her halfway. It wasn't a hot kiss—not with morning breath and the baby right there. It was something better: a promise.

When he lifted his head, the words fell out. "I love you, Rache." Her lips parted, her eyes widening, and he was struck by a terrifying sense of déjà vu as he blurted, "You don't have to say it back."

Last time she'd cracked a joke, something about how he wasn't awful—and he'd replayed that moment a thousand times in the months after she broke it off with *It's over*. He wondered, had that been the moment she decided to dump him? Or just the moment the universe had decided he was too comfortable and it was time to pull the rug out?

That tightrope feeling was back. One false step would send him plummeting and he had a nasty feeling he'd just taken that step—

But then her eyes softened, something wondering and almost awestruck lighting in them, and she whispered, "I might be somewhat fond of you too."

She kissed him, clutching his shoulders, everything in that moment—until Sofie's bright voice interrupted from the vicinity of their knees. "Mama! Hungry!"

They broke apart, grinning, and no moment had ever been more right.

Now he just had to smother that voice in the back of his head whispering that *this*, this was the moment it would all go up in flames.

CHAPTER TWENTY

The ballroom looked magnificent. The color scheme was white and gold, elegant and opulent. Perfectly matched white flocked Christmas trees with gold garland and sparkling ornaments flanked the room. Rachel studied it all with a critical eye. The Russell House logo, in glittering gold, decorated the dance floor and she subtly ran the toe of her shoe over it for the thousandth time to make sure there were no loose edges to the decals they'd used.

The dance floor was already dotted with couples in evening wear, more bejeweled women and tuxedoed men flowing through the doors all the time. The orchestra—composed of volunteers from the Denver symphony who wanted to support a good cause—played an eclectic mix of classical music, familiar holiday tunes, and popular contemporary songs, rearranged for strings.

Servers circulated with trays of canapés and champagne, but the event seemed to have escaped the fate of being stuffy and dull. Laughter rippled through the room—thanks, in large part, to the bachelors, but also to the volunteers encouraging guests to buy into the Express Pass raffle and Mystery Bags.

The alcohol was flowing and the bachelors were mingling. Each had been assigned a table to "host" for the night and some stayed close, buttering up those who had requested to be seated with them, while others worked the room.

Cam fell into the latter group, and Rachel tried not to track his movements with her eyes. She had too much to worry about tonight to be thinking about Cam. And what he'd said this morning.

Rachel caught sight of her mother, who had begged to help out. She'd had her reservations, but she had to admit Andie was doing an amazing job. All the Express Pass volunteers had been given a golden bidding paddle with a lightning bolt on it, but Andie fluttered hers like a nineteenth century courtesan, selling tickets and leaving laughter in her wake. She just hoped her mother didn't come away from the evening with another ill-fated romance.

The scene was elegant but festive, as the elite of the greater Denver area rubbed elbows—and silently compared diamond necklaces. It was exactly what Rachel had been going for. An event that would make Trista proud. This may not be her scene, this wealth and elegance, but this auction was her baby and she was going to ensure everything ran perfectly.

So far everything was going as well as could be expected. There were the usual little glitches—a bidding paddle that had been given to the wrong guest and had to be reassigned in the system, lines that were a little too long at one of the bars because the other was partially hidden by the orchestra, and pens with no ink at the silent auction tables.

If that was all that went wrong tonight, she'd count herself lucky. Reassigning paddles, redirecting guests, and replacing the pens were all easily managed.

Rachel returned a passing guest's smile, lifting one

hand to gently touch her headset as Bruno—one of her assistants for the night—spoke in her ear, asking if the veggie dinner option was vegan or just vegetarian. She moved away from the dance floor, confirming it was indeed vegan and making her way to the registration desk he was supervising in case the guest wanted more details.

After assuring that the guest's concerns had been sufficiently put to rest, she slipped back into the ballroom, scanning the room for any potential seed of a problem.

"You are a marvel," Cam said, appearing at her side. "I've already heard several people saying it's the best Russell House fundraiser yet."

Rachel slanted a look at him without stopping her perusal of the room. "Don't jinx it. The night is young."

"Come on. I thought I was the superstitious one. It's great. Take a moment to enjoy your triumph."

"I'll feel triumphant when it's over."

She loved her job, but she never actually enjoyed these events. She was too busy making sure everything ran smoothly—and noticing every tiny little detail that didn't. No one else would notice that the silent auction tables were a little too close together, making it harder for the guests to see all the items and get close enough to write their bids, but Rachel did.

"All right," Cam said. "I'll stop bugging you. But you still owe me a dance later."

He moved into the crowd, calm and confident and perfectly at ease—and she had to fight the urge to follow him with her eyes. She certainly wasn't the only one. The bachelors were all wearing gold ribbons on their lapels and there were more than a few women eyeing that ribbon, and the man it was attached to.

She'd told herself she wasn't going to be jealous—he'd made it very clear he was hers and she'd *told* him to work the crowd—but that didn't stop the scrape of anxiety beneath her skin. When he'd said he loved her this morning, the rightness of it had shivered through her, but she still hadn't been able to make herself say it back. She'd literally never said those words to a man in her life and part of her was still scared of them, even if that was exactly how she felt.

Love.

God. It was terrifying. It felt so huge. And foolish. A flying leap into the unknown—and Rachel didn't do the unknown. She liked things she could control. Things she could predict. The best laid plans. But Cam had never been one to conform to her plans.

He'd been moving the ornaments on her tree.

She'd started to accuse him of it that morning, but Sofie had distracted her. And then he'd said he loved her. But every time he came to visit Sofie or pick up Rachel at their apartment, she would notice later that a couple of her perfectly placed ornaments had migrated to a different spot on the tree. At first, she'd thought they were falling to lower branches, but then some had started falling *upward* and she'd become more and more certain it was Cam. Silently messing with her. Teasing her about her too-perfect tree.

And now every time she saw the tree, all she saw was him.

But she still didn't know what the future held. They hadn't talked about that. They'd agreed they were doing this—whatever this was—and he'd told her he loved her, but she didn't know what that meant for the next year or even the next month. All day she'd been trying not to panic over the fact that she didn't have a plan.

What would happen when the baseball season started? They hadn't even talked about whether Christmas morning would be with her family or his, or if they would even be together. She needed answers.

Unfortunately, answers would have to wait. Right now she had a job to do.

Her mother appeared at her side, already sold out of her Express Pass tickets, and Rachel went back to work.

*****

"I've bought *five* Express Pass tickets," the bubbly brunette in front of him bragged. "And if I win, I am absolutely picking you."

Cam hid his discomfort behind a smile. "You're a big baseball fan?"

"Oh, yeah, absolutely," she gushed in a way that gave him the distinct sense she didn't even know how many innings were in a game. "I'm sure whoever wins the Express Pass is going to pick you," she went on, with a little pout for the idea that she might not win it.

"You never know," Cam said. "There are some pretty amazing experiences on the auction block tonight." He kept hitting that word—*experiences*—but Bubbles here wasn't the first one tonight who seemed to want him more than the "experience."

"Yes, but they aren't with *you*."

It's for a good cause, he reminded himself as she put a flawlessly manicured hand on his sleeve. He would prefer to spend the night with Rachel, dancing with her, kissing her in the middle of the dance floor and letting all these eager women know he wasn't auctioning off the role of Mrs. Cameron Cole. But that wouldn't help the charity.

And even if he had been inclined to spend the entire night with Rachel in his arms, she wouldn't let him. This event meant too much to her. And she was too focused for that. When he'd spoken to her earlier, he'd realized that talking to her now was like someone trying to talk to him in the middle of an inning. She looked gorgeous in a simple white cocktail dress that hugged her figure and stopped just below her knees, but she was in game mode, and he needed to let her concentrate.

Which meant focusing on what he'd come here for. Raising money for Russell House. Even if it meant letting lots of women in expensive gowns squeeze his biceps.

"Cameron Cole. What's a nice boy like you doing in a place like this?"

Cam turned toward the familiar voice, the first genuine smile he'd had in hours curving his lips. "Erika. I should have known you'd be here."

His ex-wife moved in for a hug, effectively dislodging the brunette, who continued to hover nearby, clearly hoping the new arrival would depart quickly. The orchestra began *I'll Be Home for Christmas,* and Erika cocked her head as she stepped back from the hug. "I believe they're playing our song. Care to dance, Mr. Cole?"

"I'd love to."

He offered her his arm and they wove through the crowd toward the dance floor, past at least a dozen women who were eyeing him speculatively. He really hadn't taken into account how much this auction was going to make him feel like a side of beef.

Erika twirled into his arms. There were only a few couples taking advantage of the dance floor, so they at least had some privacy—even if it felt like every eye was on them.

"I don't remember this being our song," he

commented.

"You looked like you could use rescuing."

He grimaced. "Thank you." They weren't dancing so much as swaying, but it was nice to be able to relax and not have to be *on*, if only for a few minutes. "Carly and Eddie are around here somewhere. She claims she always dreamed of selling me to gypsies and this is the closest she's likely to come to realizing that dream so she wanted to be here to see it in person."

Erika laughed. "That sounds like Carly. Does she still hate me?"

"She never hated you."

Erika arched a brow.

"Okay, she hated you a little. She takes the big sister protectiveness seriously. But things have changed recently. I'd be surprised if she's still mad at you. I have a daughter now."

If they'd been doing anything more complicated, Erika would have missed a step. "Seriously?"

"I know. It caught me by surprise too."

Erika beamed. "Cam, that's great. I'm so happy for you."

"Her mom's here. Rachel. She's organizing this event. I'd love for you to meet her later. Would that be weird? I feel like you two would get along."

Her smile twisted ruefully. "Honestly, I'm just glad you're willing to let me anywhere near her."

"Well, she already found out about you the hard way." She raised a brow in question and he explained, "We started dating back when you and I were still technically married and when she found out about that things ended pretty badly. We've only just gotten back together and I'm trying not to screw it up."

"So you thought selling yourself to other women was

a good way to grow your fledgling relationship? Or is she planning on buying you tonight?"

"I don't think she's allowed to bid, since she's running the event. I signed up for this before she came back into my life—and I really didn't think there'd be so many women here. Or that they'd be so…eager."

Erika laughed. "Don't underestimate your appeal, bat boy."

"It's just hard to get excited about going on a forced date with some woman who'll have her own expectations when I'm already completely gone for the mother of my child."

"Aw." Erika smiled, something soft and wondering filling her eyes. "You're in love."

"Yeah. And I'm trying not to freak out that it's all going to go up in smoke again."

The song ended and they separated, but as Erika hooked her arm through his to leave the dance floor, she tilted her head at him. "Tell you what. I wanted to make a big donation tonight. What if I bid on you? If I win, you can take your girl instead."

"You'd do that?"

"Can you think of a better way to use the money I got in the divorce? It feels weird having it when I already owe you so much."

"You don't owe me—"

"Cam. I do. You took care of me when you didn't have to. You were my friend when a lot of people wouldn't have been able to see past the way I hurt you. I think you might be the only person on the planet who would bend over backwards to help the woman who had just dumped you."

"Dumped is kind of a harsh way of putting it," he said wryly and she laughed.

"Consciously uncoupled?"

He smiled, glad they could joke about it now, friends again. A couple years ago it hadn't been quite so easy, back when it felt like the hits just kept coming. Cancer. Divorce. "It was the right thing, us splitting up. Even if I didn't see it right away. We would have made each other miserable in the long run."

"And now we both have a chance at happiness." She smiled. "So will you let me do this for you? Call it a belated thank you gift."

"Only if it doesn't go ridiculously high. There are limits."

"Agreed." She grinned as another woman clutching a handful of Express Passes homed in on them. "Of course our plan only works if you don't get snapped up in the Express Pass round."

He groaned. "You'd think more people would want to fly a fighter plane."

"You want me to run interference?"

"No. This is what we're here for, right? And it's all for a good cause."

Erika smiled. "The best."

CHAPTER TWENTY-ONE

It's all for a good cause. That was the mantra Rachel kept repeating to herself as Cam smiled and charmed the swarm of women around him. It was harder to maintain the mantra when he was swaying with the blonde on the dance floor, laughing with her in *entirely* too familiar a way. But Rachel wasn't jealous. Nope. It was all for a good cause.

He was doing his part for charity. At least that's what she told herself. Until she overheard one of the guests speaking urgently into his cell phone as he hid behind one of the Christmas trees along the side of the room.

"Trust me, this is so much better than cancer schmaltz. Cameron Cole and his ex-wife are getting back together—"

Rachel jerked at the sentence—and the realization of why the blonde looked familiar. She wasn't in a Cameron Cole jersey this time, but she looked equally at home in the couture gown.

"The baseball player," continued the gossip columnist—since that was who the man had to be. She knew they'd invited a few society pages people to talk about the fundraiser, but she hadn't expected to overhear one practically orgasming at the thought of Cam and his wife reuniting. "I have a killer shot of the two of them gazing lovingly into each other's eyes on the dance floor. I'm surprised no one turned the fire hoses on them—"

Okay, that was a bit of an exaggeration. Yes, Cam had danced with his ex and yes, it had looked rather intimate, but fire hoses? Come on.

Rachel pushed away from the wall, walking away from the giddy reporter and his scoop. *Nothing to see here, folks.* She wasn't jealous. She trusted Cam. He was not still in love with his wife. He'd told her he loved her that morning. Yes, she had trust issues where men were concerned, but this time she wasn't going to freak out and screw everything up.

She just needed to focus on her job. The guests were settling in for the dinner service as the emcee announced the first speaker—a woman with a testimonial about how Russell House had saved her life. This was the fatten-them-up-for-the-kill portion of the evening. Lots of good food, good wine, and stories about how amazing the cause they were all there to support was. Get everyone in a happy, giving mood before the bidding started.

Rachel moved along the edge of the room, supervising the action, making sure no guests were looking irritable—and trying very hard not to notice that Cam's ex was seated right beside him at his table. Because *of course she was.*

Rachel had made the seating chart herself, but the former Mrs. Cole must go by her maiden name now because she hadn't noticed anything unusual about the names at Cole's table. And she wasn't going to read anything into it now. She was working. Concentrating on the event. Not. Jealous.

The auction began as the dessert course was served. The auctioneer was marvelous—witty and entertaining, keeping the tone light and fun and the pace fast. The announcement of the Express Pass was first. Rachel found herself holding her breath, nervous that the winner would pick Cam—though *someone* had to pick him—but when the winning number was read, a woman at the fighter pilot's table leapt to her feet, squealing, and immediately claimed the pilot's date.

There were a few disappointed groans, but more applause as the pilot came to his feet and hugged the winner. Then the auctioneer called the first bachelor up on stage. As his date was described, the rock climber played along, leaping up to catch the edge of the balcony above him and dangling lazily from one arm as the bidding began.

Rachel scanned the room. The spotters were doing well—not encouraging the bidding, but identifying the bidders and keeping their paddles raised next to the current high bidder to help the auctioneer keep track as the numbers flew higher. The guests did enough goading of one another, driving the bids up amid laughter and playful trash talking.

The paragliding adventure was won by a man and the bachelor in question met the winner at the edge of the stage for a handshake and a backslapping hug.

And the auction barreled on.

Rachel didn't want to jinx it, but the evening really was going well. A few of the patrons had opened their Mystery Bags—which they weren't supposed to do until they left the ballroom due to the contract with the hotel that forbade them from bringing in their own alcohol—but there hadn't been any major snafus.

Money was rolling in. The guests were having fun. Even the A/V equipment—which almost *always* went sideways at these events—all seemed to be working.

People would be talking about this event, which would be good for Russell House and even better for TD Events and Rachel's career. She didn't want to get ahead of herself, but as the bachelors were auctioned off one-by-one, things were looking really good.

Cam was scheduled to go last. As the designated headliner of the event, they expected him to bring in the biggest price—though some of the other dates had already claimed eye-popping amounts. Rachel stood at the back of the ballroom, clasping her hands together and trying to pretend she was totally calm as Cam's date was announced and he rose to make his way toward the stage.

He looked uncomfortable—not that most people would notice. His smile was in place, his body was relaxed—and the man looked freaking amazing in a suit. But there was something off. He was hating this—and somehow that made Rachel feel better. That knowledge that they were both miserable he was about to go to the highest bidder. Even if she hadn't been barred from bidding as an employee of TD Events, she wouldn't have been able to afford him anyway, not as the bidding quickly jumped from the hundreds to the thousands. And kept climbing.

It's for a good cause. Rachel repeated her mantra—reasonably certain Cam was repeating the same thing to himself as the bidding continued fast and furious.

Then a new paddle rose—and a ripple went around the room.

His ex had joined the bidding.

Rachel tried to keep her cool. She tried to remember that breathing was a necessary pastime. But the numbers were getting ridiculous—*ten thousand dollars for batting practice?*—and whispers were traveling around the room. Erika's identity was being passed from lip to lip.

"That's one way to win him back!" one heckler shouted, and everyone laughed.

These people knew them. This was their world. They ran in these circles—and Rachel wasn't even in the same tax bracket. She'd told herself she wasn't jealous when she'd seen them talking and dancing and laughing. She'd told herself he really wanted to be dancing with *her*. That he *would* be dancing with her at the end of the night. But that didn't make it any easier to watch the bidding as Erika and another woman really got into it.

Rachel forced her expression to remain neutral, a professional smile frozen in place. Her mother was one of the bid spotters and she could feel her looking over at Rachel every time the bidding took another leap. It wasn't like she could do anything—even if she'd wanted to jump dramatically into the bidding, they'd long since passed out of her tax bracket.

Twelve thousand.

Thirteen.

He'd told her he didn't still have feelings for his ex, but the second Erika had entered the bidding he'd looked straight at his ex-wife and smiled. A real smile. A *private* smile.

The idiot woman bidding against her didn't know she'd already lost. Cam kept smiling every time Erika trumped the other woman's paddle, his eyes glinting. Because of course *now* he was having fun. People were rooting for her now. Cheering. And Rachel was starting to feel sick.

When the final gavel fell, the ballroom erupted into applause. A freaking standing ovation. It was a lot of money. A freaking *ton* of money. More money than anyone would ever spend if they were over their ex-spouse.

It was a statement. A message. Hands off, ladies. He's still mine.

Erika glided to the edge of the stage to claim her prize.

It's just an auction, *Rachel reminded herself.* It's just for show.

If she were paranoid, she might be obsessing over the fact that Cam hadn't said he wanted a future with her. He'd just said he loved her. He'd never actually said he didn't want to get back together with his ex—but she wasn't going to be paranoid.

Until Erika stepped up on stage and some idiot in the crowd shouted, "Kiss her!"

Erika and Cam laughed, holding hands at the edge of the stage, but the crowd was relentless. It started as a chant—but then quickly became another bidding war.

"I've got a hundred for Russell House if you kiss her!"

"Two hundred!"

"I'll match that!"

The auctioneer, never one to miss an opportunity to garner more money for the charity, repeated the bids into the microphone. Cheers echoed in the room, along with more bidders chipping in, adding to the tally if Cam would kiss his ex.

Rachel silently begged Cam to defuse the situation—give her a peck on the cheek, something to silence the noisy crowd—but he laughed and swept his ex into a dramatic dip, like something out of a silent film. And the crowd went wild.

She couldn't watch this.

Not after all those secret smiles. Not after the way they'd danced. Not after she'd dropped twenty-two-freaking-thousand dollars on batting practice.

The event would survive. Her assistants had things well in hand and now that the auction was over all that was left was dancing and cashing out. She'd done her job. And she couldn't be here for this.

Rachel rushed toward a service door.

The crowd hooted and cheered en masse. That sound could only mean one thing. He'd kissed her.

He'd been boxed into a corner. She knew that. It was for a good cause. But she couldn't stop the doubts chasing one another around in her brain.

Had she been wrong to trust him? Had he lied to her again? He'd said Erika wasn't in his life anymore, hadn't he? God, why couldn't she remember his actual *words*? Men like that, men like her father, they lived in the technicalities. They weren't *really* lying, you just didn't *understand* what they *meant*. They misled. They manipulated. But that wasn't Cam, was it?

Suddenly she was questioning every word he'd ever said to her. Every look.

Rachel ducked her head as she darted out of the ballroom. She had never teared up in the middle of a job. She was a professional, damn it. She was not going to fall apart now.

The service hallway was quiet—and cold as a frozen-over hell. She shivered, wrapping her arms around herself and leaned against the basic beige wall, inhaling long and slow. The servers had finished clearing already, only the bartenders remaining active as the party began to wind down, so at least she was alone with her stupidity.

She didn't know how long she stood there. She knew she should go back to the ballroom. She needed to be monitoring the situation, watching for microexpressions of discontent so she could defuse situations before they had a chance to become problems. But she couldn't breathe.

"Rachel?"

Her mother. Of course.

She straightened away from the wall, head high and arms loose at her sides as she moved back toward the ballroom. "Thank you for your help tonight. I think you sold as many Express Passes as all the other volunteers combined."

"Rachel..." Her mother's concerned face floated in front of her, but she kept walking.

They were not going to talk about this.

"I'll be here for a while longer finishing up, but you shouldn't wait for me."

"Sweetie, I don't think he—"

She cut her mother off before she could finish that sentence. "Mom, no offense, but you don't exactly have good instincts when it comes to men."

Her mother flinched. Guilt flashed up, but Rachel was already moving past her into the ballroom—

And nearly slamming into Cam, his large frame seeming to block out the entire room.

"Hey. You ready for that dance?" He extended his hand, palm up.

As if nothing had happened. As if he hadn't just kissed his ex in front of a room full of cheering fans.

She stared at his hand, focusing on the lines and callouses. They were rough. Worn-in.

"Rachel?"

"Do you still love her?" The words were rough. Ripped from her throat. She hadn't meant to ask.

"What?" Cam laughed. "Don't be ridiculous."

Rachel's heart dropped.

He hadn't said no.

All he had to do was just say no. But men like that, they lived in the technicalities.

I love you, Andie. You know that. I've never been able to stop loving you.

But do you still love her? Do you still love your wife?

Baby, come on. Don't be ridiculous. This is you and me.

Never a denial. Never a real promise to leave her. Always evading, always *lying*.

Ice whispered through her veins, frost rippling over her skin, colder than the hallway behind her. She'd fallen in love with her father. All those broken promises. All those missed Christmases. And here she was, repeating history.

"I can't do this."

CHAPTER TWENTY-TWO

The words echoed through him, incomprehensible at first, and then seeming to grow louder in his mind, the noise from the ballroom behind him retreating as he realized what she was saying. "Rachel..."

"I can't be the other woman—"

"You aren't! That was just a stupid bachelor auction. I wanted it to be successful *for you*."

She was shaking her head, not meeting his eyes. "That's not why you kissed her. I knew I shouldn't trust you. I knew better."

And there it was. The truth. She wasn't running because of anything that had happened tonight. She'd never trusted him. Not two years ago and not now. He'd thought they were past this. He'd thought they had a chance. "I can't believe you're doing this again. Slamming the door in my face the second I tell you I love you—"

"I love you isn't a get out of jail free card," she snapped. "Do you know how often my father said that to my mother?"

"I'm not your father! I never have been!"

Rachel glanced around nervously and he became aware of the volume of his voice. They were tucked in a corner of the ballroom, far from the activity on the dance floor. Thankfully Erika's dramatic gesture had scared off all the women who'd been chasing him all night, but he hadn't expected it to scare off Rachel as well. He thought he'd earned a little more faith than that.

"I trusted you before—"

"No, you didn't," he cut her off. "If you had, you wouldn't have ghosted on me. And you wouldn't be running now. You never really let yourself believe me, and maybe you never will." She averted her eyes, not denying it, and something helpless and angry unfurled in his chest. "Were you going to leave without talking to me? What was the plan? Break up with me by text again?"

She wouldn't meet his eyes.

"I can't believe this shit. It's all in your head—"

It was the wrong thing to say. He saw that the instant the words were out of his mouth. "I have work to do," she said icily. "Goodbye, Cam."

She was leaving. She was cutting him out. Ruthlessly excising his heart from his chest. But it was different this time.

This time he had to watch her walk away.

*****

The guests were leaving. Checking out. Heading to the valet to collect their cars or catch their Ubers, if they'd had a little too much.

This was usually when she began to feel that thrill of exhilaration. The feeling that she'd done it. They'd pulled it off. All the hard work had been worth it. She should be happy.

But Rachel didn't feel any of that. She couldn't triumph in her success—and it had been a success. The numbers didn't lie. This year's fundraiser had blown previous years out of the water. Thanks in part to Cam's ex.

The orchestra was packing up, the bartenders had long since announced last call, and all but a few die-hards had left the ballroom. Cam was gone. She hadn't seen him leave, but as soon as she noticed his absence, regret had begun to whisper in her ear. Her anger had worn off and she felt *heavy*.

Rachel knew she should move out to the coat check to oversee the last departures, but instead she sank down at one of the empty tables, staring at the perfect white and gold line of perfect Christmas trees.

The expression on Cam's face—like she was the one betraying *him*—haunted her as logic started to seep through the emotion that had blinded her.

She'd been so scared to believe any man who claimed he loved her—especially when she was so vulnerable. Especially when she loved him, the emotion so big that it would eat her alive if she let it, consuming all her logic and making her do anything to stay with him.

Love made people stupid and she had to fight against that, didn't she? Stay strong? For Sofie?

Her father had been sympathetic too. Always with the perfect thing to say. Or at least that was how she remembered him. This mythical figure who kept dragging them back into his net—composed more of stories and reflections of all the other Mr. Wrongs her mother had dated than of her half-formed memories of the man himself.

As if conjured by her thoughts, her mother perched on the chair beside her. "You did it," her mother murmured.

Rachel swallowed, her gaze still on the trees. "I thought you went home."

"There was a run on the coat check. The attendants were overwhelmed so I pitched in."

Rachel looked over at her mother, tears pricking the back of her eyes. Her mother who was always there when she needed her. "Thank you for being here tonight." She reached over, linking their hands. "I'm sorry about what I said earlier."

Andie grimaced, lines Rachel had never noticed before creasing the edges of her eyes. "You weren't wrong. I'm not the best judge of men. Though, for what it's worth, I don't think he cares about that woman. I don't think he's anything like your father."

"Mom. You saw…"

"I did. And I'm not saying he wasn't an idiot. But I also saw the look on his face when you walked away. Are you sure this is what you want? Are you sure you weren't just looking for any reason to run because you were scared?"

"And if I was?" Rachel snapped, defensiveness making her voice sharp. "Can you blame me?"

"No," Andie murmured after a silent moment. "But I can blame myself."

"Mom." She shook her head.

"They say children learn about relationships from the examples in their lives, they learn what love is by example, but I always thought I could protect you from my mistakes. That they wouldn't touch you. That you would grow up to be nothing like me when it came to love."

"I did," Rachel reminded her. Her mother was too trusting, so she didn't trust. Her mother threw herself into emotion, so she held herself back.

"Did you?" her mother asked—not trying to make a point, but genuinely asking. "I let fear control me—fear of losing your father, fear of being alone. So much fear. Are you sure you aren't doing the same thing?"

Rachel tried to dismiss the idea as ridiculous. She was nothing like her mother. She was the practical one. The emotionless one. But tonight had she been driven by cool, calm reason? Or had she been falling apart in an icy hotel hallway? Had she been as foolish as she'd always silently judged her mother for being? Letting her emotions kick her brain out of the driver's seat?

"I want to believe him," she whispered. "I want to trust him, but how do I do that when everything practical and logical in me is saying I shouldn't?"

"What's your heart saying?"

It was instinctive to reject the words. It didn't matter what her heart wanted. Love didn't conquer all. No one rode off into the sunset to live happily ever after. There were no Christmas miracles. Her mother put her faith in that crap and it never worked out. How many times had she seen that? How was she supposed to ignore the evidence of a lifetime?

"He's still Sofie's father," her mother murmured when the silence had gone on too long.

"I'm not going to keep him from Sofie." But she had to be smart for Sofie. Strong for her. She wanted her baby to grow up safe and confident. Secure that she was loved and—

And not afraid of her own heart.

Tears pressed against the back of Rachel's eyes. She didn't want Sofie to be anything like her. Too scared of being hurt to let herself fall.

Someone hit the lights and suddenly the ballroom went dim, lit only by the glow of the perfect gold and white Christmas trees. They were flawless. Each ornament in place. And she hated them.

Cam had moved the ornaments on her tree at home. Messing with her. Teasing her about trying to make everything too perfect—but when she looked at those lopsided ornaments, she didn't see imperfection. She just saw him.

She'd been trying to protect herself from the messy parts of life, from the chaos she'd always ascribed to her mother's irresponsibility, but her mother had only hurt herself. Rachel had hurt a good man.

And he was a good man. She knew that. She *trusted* that.

She turned to her mother, horror washing through her. "Did I just ruin everything?"

Andie squeezed her hand. "I saw him go out on the balcony earlier. Start by groveling. It really does help."

CHAPTER TWENTY-THREE

There was a certain symmetry to ending up on the balcony. Their relationship had started on the balcony of a hotel ballroom after a fundraiser. It was only fitting that it should end on one. Everything came full circle.

Though this time instead of sharing a bottle of champagne he'd finagled from the open bar, he was alone, drinking the scotch he'd dropped two-hundred dollars on in the silent auction. And instead of an unusually warm September night, he was freezing his ass off, watching the heavy clouds that had blocked out the moon and waiting for it to snow.

Still. Symmetry. You had to appreciate that shit.

Life had a way of repeating itself.

He went after something he wanted, and the second he actually let himself believe he could get it, the second he got comfortable, the universe yanked it away. That was why he could never make himself trust that he was going to get another game, let alone another season.

When he'd been yanked from the State Championship team, after his coaches had *sworn* that reliability mattered more than talent, he'd begged for that spot, pleading with them to reconsider.

When she'd broken up with him via a freaking *text* message, he'd left countless messages, asking for an explanation. *Pleading*.

He wasn't begging again.

Cam stared into the depths of his whiskey glass, seeing the truth in the amber liquid. She was never going to trust him. It didn't matter what he did. And the sooner he got that through his thick head, the sooner he could focus on being Sofie's dad.

She wouldn't cut him off from Sofie. But would he be able to see her without wanting her? How were they supposed to get through the holidays?

Maybe he could explain. Beg her to believe him. It probably wouldn't work, but what was the point of dignity anyway?

"Are you wallowing?"

Cam jerked at the sharp female voice behind him, putting his back to the railing to face his sister. "What are you doing here?"

Carly ignored the distinct lack of welcome in his voice, crossing the balcony toward him and tugging her shawl tight around her. "Eddie and I were taking advantage of the kidless time for some bathroom sex—"

He cringed. "Thank you for that image. If you'll excuse me, I need to bleach my brain."

"And when we finally made it up to the parking lot, we saw your car." She bumped his elbow with hers. "I got worried. And obviously I was right. Since I'm always right."

"Lucky you."

"Are you going to tell me what's wrong?" When he didn't immediately spill his guts, she propped herself against the railing at his side, settling in. "I assume it's Rachel?"

"She accused me of lying again. Of getting back with Erika." He lifted his glass for another gulp of scotch. He was way beyond sipping. "I am so goddamn sick of wanting things that get snatched away. You guys keep pushing me to go after what I want and be honest about what I want and you know what happens when I do? I get kicked in the fucking teeth."

"Yes, your life is hard." Carly sighed dramatically. "When do you play the Yankees again?"

"I worked my ass off for my career," he snapped and his sister nodded.

"I know. And yet you're still terrified you don't deserve it."

"It's not about deserving it. I have to keep up the act. The second you let someone see something real, the second you're vulnerable, that's when the whole thing blows up in your face," he argued. "Just like this. Everyone says I'm the golden child, that I'm this eligible bachelor, but my wife left me the second she found out she had cancer—it was her wake-up call and what she woke up to was that she had never loved me."

"To be fair, I'm not sure you ever loved her like that either."

He spoke over her. "And now today I tell Rachel that I love her and within twenty-four hours she's gone. Just like last time. Did I tell you that? That I told her I loved her the morning before she dumped me two years ago too. How messed up is that? Everyone says I'm such a catch. Such a nice guy. Well, nice guys finish last." He toasted her with his drink and she took it out of his hand.

"That's bullshit." She downed the last swallow of scotch in the glass. "Any guy who says nice guys finish last is almost assuredly using it as an excuse to act like a dick."

"Excuse me?"

"Of course she assumed the worst. You've seen the

baggage she's lugging around. That is a steamer case of issues. Did you think that saying you love her and waving your magic penis at her was going to make them all go away?"

"Please never mention my penis again."

"I saw you flirting with Erika and I have to say, even I wondered if there were some old sparks at play there—"

"I. Wasn't. Flirting. We were just dancing—"

"During the bidding, dumbass. You were practically winking at her every time she bid. And then she got up on stage and everyone started chanting for a kiss and you could have stopped it. You could have gotten down off that stage, but you were enjoying the moment."

He turned to face the railing, gripping it and staring blindly at the city. "It wasn't romantic. It's not like that."

"I know that. But I've known you forever. Literally since you were a squalling brat. Ugliest baby on the planet. But Rachel hasn't. She's known you what? Six weeks total over the course of two plus years? You should have seen her face, Cam. When you and Erika were up on that stage. Did you even look at her?"

Shame whispered through him. He hadn't. And he had been having fun, enjoying the moment. All those people bidding on him.

"Did you ever even *talk* to her about the future?" Carly asked.

"She just came back into my life. I thought there'd be time to figure out the future later."

"Sounds like a good way to end up with two different ideas of what the future should be. And how'd that work out with Erika, again?" she asked sweetly.

"This isn't about Erika."

"No. It's about Rachel. And that girl is a planner. I

bet she has five-year plans and five-month plans and even five-day plans. And if you haven't talked to her about making a plan together, how is she going to know that's what you want?"

Cam stared out at the city. Carly wasn't wrong, no matter how much he might want her to be. He'd been doing exactly what he did the first time with Rachel—focusing so hard on making her love him so she wouldn't want to leave without telling her that he wanted her to stay. But last time she'd left anyway. She'd jumped to conclusions and shut him out.

"She'll never trust me," he said, the words defensive. "I can't make her love me."

"True. But I don't think that's the problem." Carly rolled the empty scotch glass between her hands. "I will deny this if you ever repeat it, but you're a pretty damn lovable guy. And I'm pretty sure she's freaking nuts about you—which probably scares her even more than it scares you. Give her time. Have a little faith in her. It's not always about you and your delicate male ego."

"Thank you for that beautiful speech," he said dryly, but her words were whispering around in his brain, reshaping the night.

"What can I say? I'm like a walking cheesy Christmas movie." She shoved away from the railing. "Come on. My poor sex-exhausted husband has probably fallen asleep waiting for us inside. Let me wake him up and then I'll drive you home." His sister, the world's horniest Christmas elf.

Cam didn't move. "I love you, you know that?"

"Yeah, yeah. You had me at hello and all that shit."

"But, really, you can stop telling me about your sex life anytime."

Carly laughed. "Where's the fun in that?"

She opened the door and Eddie looked up from his phone. "All done?" he asked—and Cam tried very hard not to think about what his sister and brother-in-law had or hadn't done in the bathroom earlier.

"You bet," Carly announced. "I was brilliant."

Cam snorted, still leaning against the railing. "I might just get a room down here. Head home tomorrow."

Carly opened her mouth to argue—then her gaze slid to the side and she did the unprecedented thing of shutting up, so Cam had subconsciously already braced himself when Rachel appeared in the doorway holding a bottle of champagne.

"Hey." Her expression cautious, she lifted the bottle. "I brought a peace offering."

His heart wanted to leap toward her, but he stamped it down, gripping the railing behind him.

"I'm sorry," she said, stepping out onto the balcony. "I know it seemed like I didn't trust you, but it was me I didn't trust. I've never wanted to fall in love. It always seemed like an excuse to behave stupidly and I wanted to be smarter than that. You made me feel stupid—because I loved you." She glanced down, biting her lip, and when she raised her eyes, his heart stopped. "I love you. You screw up my Christmas tree and complicate my life, but I love you, Cam. I can't imagine a perfect Christmas without you."

He was frozen, waiting for the *but* when she went on. "It was never about your ex, but when you kissed her—"

"I'm sorry." Suddenly the words rushed out. "I was an ass, playing it up for the crowd—"

"I *told* you to."

"We have no feelings for one another. Not like that," he swore. "She bought the date for us. So we could go on it together. As a way of thanking me for supporting her when she was sick and supporting Russell House at the same time."

Rachel's eyes rounded. "She did?"

"We're just friends now. I swear." He pushed away from the railing, closing the distance between them. It had started snowing but he was barely aware of the flakes melting on his skin. "Anything romantic between us was over a long time ago. You're it for me, Rache."

"You're it for me too," she whispered, the words choking. And then she was in his arms, squeezing him tight, holding on for dear life. "I'm so sorry," she said again, her voice muffled by his coat as she pressed her face into his shoulder. "I was scared to want anyone as much as I wanted you. I thought you'd have this mystical power over me if I let myself love you and I was terrified to trust anyone that much. To need you more than I need my good sense or self-respect. I was looking for any excuse to run, to save myself—but I don't want to run. I don't want to lose you."

Relief shattered him as he cupped her face. "You don't have to. I'm not going anywhere. I told myself I wasn't going to beg, but I wouldn't have lasted one day. I need you too much. I want us. You and me and Sofie." He brushed his thumb along the silky softness of her cheek. "I love you, Rachel. Do you believe me when I say that?"

"I'm learning to." Her eyes glistened, tears mixing with the snowflakes melting on her cheeks. And then—finally—he kissed her.

It was a Christmas miracle—the taste and feel of her in his arms, the feeling that she wasn't going anywhere, that this thing between them would only continue to grow. He could have stayed there kissing her on the balcony all night if it hadn't been for the cold and the snow.

And his sister.

"That is so stinkin' cute. How come you never profess your undying love to me anymore, Eddie?"

Cam broke the kiss, glowering over Rachel's shoulder at his sister. "Did you seriously just stand there watching all that?"

"You bet. All we needed was a little popcorn and it would have been better than a rom-com. Just wait, when you have as many kids as we do, you gotta take your chances for date night wherever you can. Hotel bathrooms..."

"Stop. Please. There isn't enough brain bleach in the world to make me want to hear the rest of that sentence."

"See you Christmas morning, Rachel!" Carly called as Eddie half-dragged her inside, the door slamming shut behind them.

Cam returned his full attention to the woman in his arms. "I've heard worse ideas," he murmured.

"Christmas morning?"

"That. And half a dozen kids running around. I was thinking we should start making plans."

"For half a dozen kids? I was thinking more like four."

He grinned. "Yeah?"

"Though we'll need a nanny since I'm not giving up event planning. Maybe we can hire my mom full time."

He grinned. "I like that plan."

Her eyebrows arched. "I thought you were anti-plan."

"I love your plans." He couldn't think of anyone he'd rather make plans with. "They're one of my favorite things about you. I just don't want you to miss the scenery along the way."

She eyed him up and down. "It is pretty decent scenery."

"Pretty decent?"

She shrugged, her lips twitching. "Tolerable."

"*Tolerable*?"

"Moderately appealing."

She shrieked out a laugh as he swept her up into his arms, carrying her toward the door. "I'll show you tolerable."

The champagne bottle she still clutched in one hand bounced against his back. "Where are we going?"

"To get a room. Unless we need to get home for Sofie. In which case, I hear there's a bathroom near here..."

EPILOGUE

Five years later…

Rachel held her breath as she closed the door to the nursery, sending up a silent plea to any deity who was listening for a full night's sleep. The twins seemed to have developed a tag-team system and she was seriously considering begging her mother to come back as a night nanny just so she and Cam could get eight solid hours. Or even six. Hell, she'd settle for three.

She padded silently toward the great room, the sound of muffled giggling alerting her there was something afoot even before she rounded the corner and saw them.

Cam stood next to the tree, his hand incriminatingly close to the ornaments. "See the trick is to just move them a little," he was intoning like a Harvard lecturer. "That way she isn't a hundred percent certain they're out of place and you can slowly move them around the tree."

Rachel paused at the edge of the room and smothered a grin, waiting until Cam had Milo's silver baby's first Christmas ornament firmly in his hand before she folded her arms across her chest and called out, "I knew it! Caught red-handed."

Cam whirled. "It's the fuzz! Hide the evidence!"

He shoved the ornament behind his back. Milo and Cassidy squealed, ducking behind their father's legs while Sofie, with the lofty maturity of her six-and-a-half years, merely slapped a hand over her mouth to smother her giggles, her eyes glinting wickedly. Of all their kids, she was the most like her father—and the most likely to be lured into one of his schemes.

Rachel approached, shaking her head direly, playing her part to the hilt. "Not only are you defiling my Christmas tree, you're corrupting our sweet, innocent children."

The cherubs in question giggled helplessly as Cam held up the baby spoon. "I'll have you know that Milo's baby ornament *fell* and I was valiantly returning it to its place of honor."

"Mm-hm." She held out her hand, palm up, and he sighed dramatically before slapping the silver spoon onto it. She turned to the tree, eyeing it to see how much damage he'd already done.

It wasn't the same tree she'd had when they met. They got fresh trees every year now—but she still spent the most time decorating. Getting it just right. Shifting things around until it was perfect.

And every year Cam messed with her ornaments whenever she wasn't looking. Though as far as she knew, this was the first time he'd turned the kids into his partners in crime.

She'd worried, when he announced last year that he wanted to retire from baseball and be a stay-at-home dad, that he would be bored. She hadn't counted on him turning their offspring into his willing accomplices—though Cassidy could always be relied upon to tattle to her. Cassidy loved rules. That one was definitely *her* baby.

They were in Boulder full time now—which was a relief now that Sofie was in school. Winters in Boulder and baseball season in LA had been a challenge. Rachel had gone to part time at TD Events, with a few breaks for maternity leave, but now she was back to full time. Cam had started encouraging her to start her own company, but for now she was happy where she was. She'd talked to Trista about the toll the company had taken on her home life when she was building her business and Rachel had no interest in putting her kids through that. Maybe someday, but she wasn't in a hurry. For once, she didn't need a five year plan. The present was pretty damn perfect already.

She hung the spoon back in its place and Cam sighed dramatically. "You're a little bit of a tree dictator, you know that?"

"I just like order and efficiency," she said, the kids all grinning at the familiar refrain. "There's a system."

"Uh-huh." Cam reached out in slow motion, his eyes locked on hers the entire time, and grabbed the spoon, moving it to a branch two inches to the left. Much too close to the Jingle Bell Santa.

Rachel narrowed her eyes. "Seriously?"

"I just want to see how long you can go before you move it back."

She held his eyes, putting steel into her gaze, determined not to crack.

She lasted five minutes.

Her opportunity came when Cam shooed the kids down the hall for bedtime. "Get moving, team. Pajamas for everyone. Teeth to be brushed. Stories to be read."

As he herded the kids toward their bedrooms, Rachel took advantage of his distraction to quickly move the spoon back.

Cam's arms closed around her from behind before she could lower her hand. "Caught red-handed," he murmured against her hair.

She leaned back against him, folding her arms over his. She'd never believed in love at first sight—until she saw Cam. And Sofie. And Cassidy and Milo and the twins. She'd thought love made you stupid, that it made a person do things that made no earthly sense—until she'd figured out that love was what made *everything* make sense. It was the logic and the explanation. And five years into her happily ever after, she was starting to think love might just conquer all.

The right kind of love. With the right kind of man. Like the one who had burst into her life and disrupted all her plans.

"I love this tree," she said, staring up at the branches from the circle of Cam's arms. "I think the Battle of the Tree might be my favorite part of Christmas."

"You know what my favorite part of Christmas is?" he asked.

She looked up at him over her shoulder. They knew each other so well now, after five years of ups and downs, arguing and making up. She trusted him completely, down to her soul, but he was still surprising her every day. "What?"

"You. You're the best Christmas gift I ever got."

"Aw." She turned in his arms, grinning and tipping her face up for a kiss. "That was so sappy. I love it. When the kids are in bed, you wanna put on a cheesy Christmas movie and cuddle for five whole minutes before we both pass out from exhaustion?"

Cam laughed, his arms squeezing her close. "Sounds like a plan."

Thank you for reading *AN UNPLANNED CHRISTMAS*. If you enjoyed the book, please consider leaving a review at your favorite bookseller or book club website.

To meet Rachel's brother, don't miss ***THE DECOY BRIDE*** from the Bouquet Catchers series.

For more holiday romance, look for the other books in Lizzie Shane's Yours For Christmas series: *ALL HE WANTS FOR CHRISTMAS* and *MIRACLE ON MULHOLLAND.*

ABOUT THE AUTHOR

Award-winning contemporary romance author Lizzie Shane lives in Alaska where she uses the long winter months to cook up happily-ever-afters. A three-time finalist for Romance Writers of America's prestigious RITA Award, she also writes paranormal romance under the pen name Vivi Andrews. Find more about Lizzie or sign up to receive her newsletter for updates on upcoming releases at www.lizzieshane.com.

ALSO BY LIZZIE SHANE

MARRYING MISTER PERFECT
ROMANCING MISS RIGHT
FALLING FOR MISTER WRONG
PLANNING ON PRINCE CHARMING
COURTING TROUBLE
ALWAYS A BRIDESMAID
LITTLE WHITE LIES
DIRTY LITTLE SECRETS
ALL HE WANTS FOR CHRISTMAS
THE DECOY BRIDE
MIRACLE ON MULHOLLAND
THE REAL THING

Made in the USA
Las Vegas, NV
15 December 2021